GW01236745

AVENGE THE DARKNESS

A Post Apocalyptic EMP Survival Thriller

RYAN CASEY

GET A POST APOCALYPTIC NOVEL FOR FREE

To instantly receive an exclusive post apocalyptic novel totally free, sign up for Ryan Casey's author newsletter at: ryancaseybooks.com/fanclub

CHAPTER ONE

A oife looked at the blood on her hands, dripping through her fingers.

She felt hot. So hot. Her teeth chattered. Her whole body felt weak, shaky. It was cold. Bitter cold, so cold it hurt to breathe. Her lips were chapped, and her fingers were numb.

But she didn't feel cold.

Before her, grass.

Grass that she didn't want to look at.

A patch of grass up ahead that she knew wasn't frozen, like the rest of the ground. Far from frozen.

But in her mind, she could already see the scene before her. Even if she didn't want to look at it. Even if she didn't want to admit it. Accept it.

Above, she heard crows cawing. The sound of death. She could hear something else, too. Panting. Heavy panting. Someone crying. Someone begging.

Maybe it was her. She wasn't sure.

It felt like she was outside her body, and this wasn't really happening.

Like she was witnessing everything from someplace outside.

She could smell something. Something strong. Something familiar.

Burning.

And that smell of burning made her sick. Because of what it reminded her of. What it took her back to.

That charred smell.

That taste of...

No.

She didn't want to go back there.

She didn't want to think about that.

She just stared at the icy ground beside her.

Tried to ignore the smell of smoke.

Tried to ignore the cloud appearing overhead.

The warmth.

The sound of flickering.

Of shouting.

Crying.

Screaming.

She didn't want to look.

She couldn't look.

She couldn't face it. She couldn't accept it.

It couldn't be real.

She heard whining over to the left. Looked around, instinctively. Because she knew that whine. She'd heard it so many times before.

When she looked around, she saw Rex standing there.

Tail between his legs.

Ears lowered.

Barely even looking at her.

Shaking.

She wanted to go over to him. To cuddle him. To comfort him.

She wanted to feel comfort from him.

But she felt frozen.

Frozen here on this patch of grass.

The ice beneath her bloodied fingers melting.

The air growing warmer as that flickering sound grew louder.

"It's okay," she muttered. Voice shaking. "Everything... everything's going to be okay."

She looked into Rex's eyes.

Saw the orange glow flickering in those deep black sockets.

Saw it reflecting the whole scene back to her.

And at that moment, she felt herself being transported back.

Back to that day six months ago.

Back to that moment.

Back to that decision.

She tensed her fists. Her fingers dug right into her palms. The heat from behind grew stronger. So hot now that her back felt like it was burning. If she stayed here much longer, it might just swallow her whole. Burn her alive.

And maybe that would be better.

Maybe that's what she wanted.

Maybe that's what would be best for everyone.

She saw Rex standing there. Panting. Tongue dangling out. Whining. Backing up. Looking at her, then looking around, like he was begging her to come after him. Begging her to follow.

And she wanted to.

She wanted to, so badly.

But she couldn't move.

She couldn't leave this place.

She couldn't walk away.

She looked down at her hands. Saw the blood on her palms. Deep red, burrowing right into the crevices.

She heard more screams behind her. Agonised cries. The kind of cry a human being shouldn't physically be able to make.

She heard it, and she closed her burning, stinging eyes.

The heat growing more intense.

Her lungs filling with smoke, making her cough and gag.

It was so close to swallowing her up now.

So close to engulfing her.

She heard barking. Looked around. Already, the smoke was thick. Black. So black she could barely even see through it.

But she could see Rex still standing there.

Barking at her.

Kicking back.

"Go," *she muttered.* "*It's okay, boy. It's okay. Go.*"

He barked some more. Kept on looking around, like there was a way to get to her. Like there was a way he could help.

But that help never did come.

"*I'm sorry. I'm so sorry.*"

She saw him step into the smoke, and just for a moment, she thought he might come running towards her.

But then he stepped back.

He disappeared.

Into the smoke.

Into the black.

Gone.

She crouched there, head spinning. A minor sense of relief that Rex had run. That he'd saved himself.

But then that relief turned into fear again.

Into shame again.

Because the patch on the grass...

She closed her eyes. Squeezed them shut. Tight.

She didn't want to look.

She didn't want to see.

But how could she not?

She owed it to them.

She owed it to all of them.

She felt her teeth chattering, her head getting dizzier, her muscles getting weaker.

Don't look, Aoife. Don't look. Just let the smoke take you. Let the heat take you. Let...

And then, against all logic, she turned.

She couldn't see much through the thick black smoke. So thick that particles felt like they were wedging into her eyes, stinging them with their heat.

Turning around, she felt like she was in a sauna. A sauna that was getting hotter and hotter and wasn't cooling down for anything.

Her chest was tight.

She couldn't breathe.

But she could see.

Not just the flames.

Not just the chaos before her.

But she could see it.

The mound on the ground, up ahead.

She looked at it, and she felt like she'd been kicked in the stomach.

Because even though she already knew what she was going to see here... just seeing it again brought the reality crashing back.

She stared ahead. Stared as the smoke got thicker. Tears streaming. Body shaking. Breathing getting even tougher, more strained.

And as she looked at that mound on the patch of grass ahead, she could only stare.

"I'm sorry. I'm... I'm so sorry."

She watched as the mound disappeared behind smoke.

Felt the heat get more intense.

Felt the burning smoke seep even further into her lungs.

And then she felt nothing.

CHAPTER TWO

A oife knew she'd fucked up the second she saw Hailey handing Max a present.

Fuck. It was his birthday. It was his frigging birthday, and she'd totally forgotten. What kind of a friend was she? He was the most important damned person in her life, and she'd gone and forgotten.

It was early, and the streets were filled with the usual bustle of morning. She could hear laughter and conversation. The sound of metal being banged up ahead as construction on the south wall continued. It'd been damaged by a nasty storm a couple of weeks back. A real blow because the first wall took a hell of a while to put together.

But did they mope about it? Let it get them down? Did they hell.

They just got right back up and cracked on with it.

Everybody got up early these days. The malaise of summer had lifted, and now winter was here, it seemed like everybody was on board with pulling their weight in this community.

The ground was icy, slippery. The air was cold. Aoife's face felt freezing. Her lips felt numb.

But you know what?

It was nice.

Nice, because despite the lack of power, there was a growing air of hope. Not about power returning, or about anyone coming to save them, or anything far-fetched like that. They'd all pretty much given up on hope of salvation a long time ago. And life had been better for it, in all truth.

No, it was nice for a few simple reasons.

Christmas was on its way.

As too was New Year.

Okay, so the thought of New Year approaching so rapidly was a weird one. It marked a year since the day the blackout struck, after all. So many people lost their lives on that day and the days that followed. And for that reason, it would likely be a very sombre occasion. Not the typical New Year's Eve blow-out, that was for sure.

But Aoife didn't mind that. Nobody here seemed to mind that.

They were going to have as nice a Christmas as they possibly could, and they were going to see in the New Year whatever way seemed appropriate when the time came.

But right now, Aoife had bigger fish to fry.

She could see Hailey and Max smiling. Laughing together. Hailey flicking back her hair. Max smirking back at her. Fuckers. Hailey was a bitch, and she didn't like her. How much of that was down to the blatant flirting between her and Max, she wasn't sure...

No.

Grow the hell up, Aoife.

Max is older than you. Okay, he might only be in his late forties, and she might only be like, a decade younger than him. But there's still a big enough gap that he's out of bounds.

Besides. He's practically a father figure. Anything happening with Max... it'd just be weird.

She thought back to that moment six months ago.

When he was on his knees.

Christopher's blade in her hands.

What she told him.

What he told her.

I love you.

She thought about how many times she'd wanted to act on that feeling since.

But she hadn't. Neither of them had.

And now here was Hailey, similar age to Max, flirting the hell away with him...

It wasn't about jealousy. Really, it wasn't.

But she'd be damned if Hailey got him a present and she didn't.

She went to turn around, confident he hadn't seen her yet. If she could get away, she could go find something for him. What? Oh, fuck, she didn't have a clue.

But she'd think of something. They had history, after all. They went back a long way.

Maybe tell him you love him.

That thought. Out of nowhere. Making her cheeks burn.

Could she?

Could she actually go there?

A knot in her stomach.

She suddenly felt very, very sick at the thought.

No.

She couldn't go there.

But she still had to get the hell away and find him a present. It was his birthday, after all. And she was supposed to be... well. His friend?

She saw him laughing, smiling, as he stood on the corner of the street just before the newly constructed south wall. Wasn't exactly the biggest construction. Twenty feet high, solid steel, with a watch platform erected along the edge of it. Not that they had visitors to worry about. Didn't seem like there was anybody about these days, apart from the odd straggler.

She went to turn around so she could head back when she saw his eyes meet her.

She kept on turning. Turning through the awkwardness. Turning like she hadn't seen him.

And then she heard his voice.

"Aoife."

She stopped. Shit. She was really in deep shit now. She couldn't exactly pretend she hadn't seen him or heard him. That'd just look weird. Especially on his birthday.

But she stayed standing there. Looking ahead. Feeling like a frigging weirdo.

"Aoife?"

She turned around. Smiled. Maybe a little too enthusiastically, especially since Hailey was looking at her, scanning her head to toe in that judgemental way she always did.

Like Aoife was a fucking child or something.

"Hey," Aoife said. Her voice cracking a bit. "Happy birthday!"

Max smiled. He looked well. A lot greyer than when they'd first met, and thinner too. But then everybody was thinner these days. Not that food was scarce—actually, things were really good on that front. Plenty of hunting teams. Scavenging missions, which were always fruitful. More than enough to feed the fifty-one residents of the estate.

"Thanks," Max said. "Hailey here got me something."

"Oh," Aoife said. "I—I got you something too."

"Ah, really? Lucky me, huh?"

Aoife nodded. Shitting hell. Why didn't she just tell the truth?

Instead, she stood there really awkwardly while Max opened the present Hailey got him, with nothing in her hands. Like an awkward bloody kid.

"I got the wrapping paper myself from an old shop in

Leyland," Hailey said, with that high-pitched nasally whine of hers. "Tried a few other places. But nothing seemed... right."

Bitch.

She nodded, smiled, watched as Max opened the gift.

And when he finally opened it... Aoife saw his eyes light up.

"Oh hell," Max said. "That's... that's actually really good."

"You sound surprised," Hailey said.

"Look at this, Aoife. Hailey draws. Hasn't she done a good job?"

Aoife didn't want to appear too praising. But looking at this pencil drawing of a dog, presumably Rex... Aoife had to admit it was actually pretty good.

"What's it supposed to be?" Aoife asked.

"Rex," Max said. "At least I'm assuming so, right?"

"Of course," Hailey said. "What else would it be?"

"I don't know," Aoife said. "Sort of looks like a cow to me. But good effort!"

Hailey narrowed her eyes.

Yeah, well, I can narrow my eyes too, you stupid bitch.

"Thanks, Hailey," Max said, going in for a hug.

And then something else happened.

Something that took Aoife by surprise.

The hug became a kiss.

On the lips.

And they held each other for just a little longer than was comfortable.

Aoife looked at the ground. Her face felt hotter than ever. She was roasting under this thick parka.

And silly as it sounded, she knew she had to get away.

"Anyway," Aoife said, turning around and walking away. "I... I'll see you later."

"What about my present?" Max asked.

You can fuck your present.

"I'll bring it you later. I—shit!"

She slipped.

Almost lost her footing on the ice.

She prayed they hadn't seen her.

But then she heard their laughs.

Max.

And Hailey, too.

That annoying frigging laugh grating right on her.

"Watch yourself," Max said. "It's a bit slippery."

Aoife gritted her teeth. "Yeah. Yeah, I know."

She got her balance back, and then she walked away from Max and Hailey with her head down.

She didn't stop fucking walking, even when she reached the gates.

CHAPTER THREE

Max watched Aoife disappear down the street, and he knew something was wrong. Right away.

It was frosty. Cold. The kind of day he might've moaned about a while ago. But truth be told, these colder mornings were beginning to grow on him. He enjoyed waking up, going downstairs, and feeding Rex. Enjoyed sitting on his doorstep and watching the sun rise. Might be getting soft in his old age, but he was really starting to feel grateful for every damned moment.

Okay. Definitely getting soft in his old age.

"What's up with her?"

He looked around. Hailey stood by his side. She was nice. Good looking woman. And she seemed to like spending time with him. She was good company. They had a laugh together.

But he could see from the way she was scowling towards Aoife that there was some kind of antagonism there.

"I'm sure she's fine."

"Do you think she has a problem?"

"A problem with what?"

"With... well. With us?"

Oh shit. Max looked away. Because as much as he liked

Hailey, as much as he appreciated her friendship and her company... he definitely wasn't looking for anything like that. Anything serious.

There was no way he was ever going to settle down like that after Kathryn. Not in a "it'd be a betrayal" way or anything like that. Or because he feared connection—because he didn't. Not anymore. He'd made a bunch of friends this last year. Some real good friendships.

He was just happy the way things were. For the first time in years, he actually felt... comfortable. At peace.

"Hailey..." Max said, preparing for the most awkward damned conversation he'd had in a while. "Don't get me wrong. You're nice, and I like you."

"Well, that's convenient," she said, placing a hand on his chest. "I like you too."

Shit. Ambushed. "I like you. But I'm... I'm really not looking for taking things any further. Like, things are good as they are. For me, anyway. I'm sorry."

He saw the way her eyes narrowed. That scowl that was reserved for Aoife just moments ago was directed at him now, just for a second.

She pulled her hand away. Looked at the icy pavement between them. "Oh."

Shit. She sounded upset. Was he a dick? Hell, he'd not gone in for that kiss. She'd just sort of... well, *planted* it on his lips.

Should he have backed away?

Hell, how old was he again? A teenager?

"I'm sorry," Max said. "The gift is great. Really. You went to a lot of effort."

Hailey nodded. Shrugged. "I'm glad you like it."

He could detect sarcasm in her voice. It irked him a bit. He knew taking the moral high ground probably wasn't the smartest move right now. But if she'd given him this gift with conditions... it felt a little off.

"Look," Max said. "You're a great friend. And I'd like it to stay that way."

"You kissed me."

"I... I think *you* kissed me. To be fair."

Hailey sighed, shook her head. "It's her, isn't it?"

Well. That was unexpected. "Who?"

"Oh, don't give me that crap. Who do you think?"

He knew who she meant. And that made it all the more awkward. Because by admitting he knew who Hailey meant... it sort of signalled she was right.

He glanced up the street. He couldn't see Aoife anymore. Just a couple of folks carrying an artificial Christmas tree towards their house, little kid with a red woolly Santa hat running between them.

"I get it," Hailey said. "I'm not as young as her. Not as pretty as her."

"No," Max said. "It's... it's really not about that."

"Then what is it?"

That stubborn old part inside Max who reigned supreme before the blackout might've told Hailey to keep her nose out once upon a time.

But she was sweet. He kind of felt he owed her an explanation.

"When my wife died. Kathryn. I... It took me a long, long time to get over her."

"I'm sorry," Hailey said.

"No need to apologise. But it's just... I think I convinced myself I'd never meet anyone again. And I was pretty set on that. And then... and then Aoife wandered into my life, and something just felt different. Not in a romantic way. Still pretty dead set on that. But she... Well. She made me realise a few things. About people. About letting people in, not pushing them away."

"Then if that's the case," Hailey said. "If you really took a leap of faith because of what she told you. Why not take another?"

Max looked at Hailey, and he had to admit she was gorgeous. Slim. Beautiful glowing skin. And she was the kind of person he could have a laugh with. That he could enjoy the company of. Way too good-looking for him, anyway.

He wanted to kiss her. To return her kiss and throw himself into the deep end.

But then just the thought of that made him feel guilty.

And it wasn't because of Kathryn.

It was because of Aoife.

He put a hand on Hailey's shoulder. Squeezed it, tight.

"Thanks for the present," he said. "Really, I love it. I'll let you know Rex's feedback as soon as I get it. I'd better, um..."

Hailey opened her mouth like she was going to say something else.

Then she nodded and very visibly sighed, cold air steaming before her. "Happy birthday, Max. You have a good one."

She turned around, shoulders slumped, walked off down the icy street.

Max watched her walk away.

Take a leap of faith. Take...

Then he sighed.

Turned around and followed in Aoife's footsteps.

CHAPTER FOUR

Three months earlier...

Grace waded down the street that looked like every other and knew it was almost time.

The roads were all the same. Cars stuck in the middle of the road. Windows smashed, glass covering the concrete. The buildings around her looked familiar, too. Little independent coffee shops. Betting shops. Takeaway after takeaway.

All the same.

Shutters down.

If the shutters weren't down, the windows were smashed.

Some of them were boarded up. Some of them had graffiti scrawled across the front. *I have a child. Help.*

And seeing them now... it pained Grace to think how desensitised she felt to it all.

This graffiti.

All the signs that this had been a bustling little community, once upon a time.

Gone.

Up ahead, she saw crows swooping down. Heard a few of them cawing in the distance. And that gave her hope. Usually, where there were birds, there was food.

And where there was food, there were people.

What she'd give to find someone right now.

She walked up this street. There was a slight incline to it. She would've had no trouble with it once upon a time. She was only twenty-three, after all, and she wasn't exactly unfit. Not the healthiest person in the world, sure. Definitely not spent enough time at the gym back in the day, and far too much money on takeaways.

She got a sudden taste of McDonald's in her mouth. The juicy burger. The salty tang of the chips. All washed down with a nice creamy helping of banana milkshake...

What she'd give for that now.

She felt weak. Her knees ached. Her feet were sore. Well, somewhere between sore and numb. The frost was so intense it felt like it was biting her toes. Her fingers weren't much better. Neither was the rest of her body.

She couldn't remember the last time she'd felt truly warm.

She stopped.

Butterflies fluttered around her stomach and chest.

She could feel her heart racing.

Her breathing getting harder, more effortful.

Keep your cool, Grace. Don't let it take you away. You've got this. You're okay.

But that memory.

The warmth.

The...

She shook her head. "No. No need to go there. Just keep walking. Just... just keep going."

She started walking again. The cracked concrete was so icy, so slippery, that she wasn't making as much progress as she wanted to. She needed to find food. She needed to find shelter.

And she needed to find people.

But not just any old people...

The memory crept up on her again.

The warmth.

The shouting.

She needed to find *them*.

She walked further up this icy slope when she felt a twinge across her face. Something sharp, something painful.

She reached her fingers to her skin when she felt it.

The ridges.

The scaliness...

She pulled her hand away, right away.

She didn't want to feel her face.

Touch her skin.

She didn't want to remember.

She stopped. Leaned against an old silver BMW. Sat there as the icy wind blew right down the length of this street. It was peaceful here. A nice little market town. She looked down to the bottom of the hill of the main street and pictured how bustling it might've been, once upon a time. Pictured the kids running out of school. The sound of them playing in the playground. The bars, crammed with people at night. The taste of beer on her lips.

She thought of it all, and then she let it go.

She couldn't dwell on the past.

The past was gone.

She got up off the car and headed further up the slope when she noticed something.

Crows. Two of them. Right by the side of the road, on a grassy verge up ahead.

She slowed down. They were scrapping over something.

And the only things crows tended to scrap about?

Food.

She moved faster. Couldn't remember the last time she'd eaten. Days ago, it had to be.

But she knew when she began this journey that sacrifices would have to be made.

She knew when she began this journey that it wasn't going to be easy. It might just kill her.

But it was worth it.

In the end, it would be worth it to find a community.

She climbed the steps leading up to the library grounds, where the crows were congregated, and she chased them away.

The crows flew off, and Grace saw what they were eating.

It was a dog. Dead dog. Looked like a border terrier. Small. Tongue dangling out. Flies buzzing around it. Smelled bad. Sour.

Grace sighed. A few hours earlier, and she could've salvaged something from this. But it smelled bad, and the flies were off-putting.

Hell. She'd eaten worse.

But this was beyond hope.

She'd have to keep on going. Have to keep on hoping.

There would be some kind of shelter nearby soon.

And hopefully, one very particular kind of shelter nearby soon.

The exact one she was looking for.

She looked down at that border terrier, and she saw a crow land a few feet away. Approach nervously, then back off.

"It's okay," Grace said. "It's all yours."

She turned around and walked away.

When she looked back, the crows from before were back, jostling over the purple flesh. The wormlike intestines. The eyes.

"Poor dog," Grace said.

She looked back down the street, back in the direction she'd come from. Over at the hills in the distance. And as much as she didn't exactly live a life of luxury, she knew she should probably just go back there. Because she had shelter there. And she knew where the best places to hunt were.

But then the memory hit her again.

And she knew she was on the right path.

She took a deep breath, the crows' caws echoing down the street, and she turned to the other side of the road to continue her journey.

That's when she heard movement.

Turned around and saw her.

She wasn't alone.

She saw who it was, and she could barely believe her luck.

She resisted the urge to go running towards her. To go after her.

She had to keep her composure.

Keep her calm.

She had to follow her.

She had to watch her closely.

And she knew exactly what she had to do next.

CHAPTER FIVE

Aoife walked aimlessly down the narrow country lane.

She didn't know why she was out here, really. Figured she'd just stretch her legs and get some fresh air. She liked walking beyond the community gates. Enjoyed being alone in the world outside. As much as things were good at the estate, she felt more comfortable when she was alone with her thoughts sometimes.

Either that, or she was just irrationally pissed at Max.

Acting like a jealous bitch.

She stopped. Thought back to the way Hailey reached up and kissed him on the lips. How watching that gross display had made her feel, deep inside.

Angry?

Bitter?

Jealous?

Fuck if she knew. But one thing was for sure: no matter how she dressed it up, she didn't feel good.

She kicked at a patch of ice on the road. Grabbed branches from the tall hedges beside her. She knew she was acting like a child. A jealous little teenage girl. What was she actually gaining by being out here, moping away?

At the end of the day, Max was a grown man. Older than her. Hailey was probably more in the old bastard's age category, anyway.

And even so... Aoife had forgotten his birthday. So it wasn't exactly a great endorsement of her character, was it?

She stopped. Sighed. Listened to the crows making that annoying sound in the sky above her. Felt the icy cold breeze against her face. Took deep breaths of it, tried to calm herself down. Mindfulness was a trick she'd learned years ago, but it was Max who'd helped her out with it recently. Who'd really awoken her to its full potential and limitless possibilities in the months she'd been coming off the booze.

Watch the breath.

Just watch the breath.

Everything else that appears is just an object, just an appearance in consciousness.

It isn't *you*.

It doesn't define you.

She kept on focusing on those breaths, letting thoughts and feelings pass like clouds in the sky, and before she knew it, she felt that inner place of calm. That place of peace, beyond everything else.

She knew a way to put being out here to good use.

She walked down the road, then took a left into the fields. The grass was crisp with frost. Icy. So cold her ears felt like they were sitting in blocks of ice. Her plan was simple: she'd forgotten Max's birthday, so she'd go into the nearest town of Longridge and get him a gift from there.

She had no idea what. But she was sure she'd find something sentimental, something that sparked a memory between them.

She walked right across the fields until eventually she saw the old Sainsbury's in the distance. And beyond that, the terraced houses of the small town. She needed to be careful. She was pretty sure there was nobody around here—their regular scouting missions confirmed that—but you could never be too certain.

Besides, stray dogs were a big problem these days. Not the fluffy friends they used to be. The ones who'd made it this far had fully reverted to their wolflike, pack instinct.

Much the same as people, really.

Only the strong and the ruthless survived.

She approached the town from higher ground, slowly. Made her way down the least residential ways possible. Through an old caravan park, filled with static caravans. It was eerie. Seeing the caravans, mostly abandoned because nobody was here at New Year when the power went out. The empty playground, a swing dangling to the wooden frame by just one metal chain. Overgrown grass.

She kept going until she reached the town of Longridge. It was always a quiet town, right in Ribble Valley about five miles from Preston, the nearest city. She'd been a few times to the little independent cinema here, which was always super nice.

Now, it was boarded up. Empty. Abandoned. Just like everywhere else.

She walked down the street, broken glass cracking underfoot. The sound of empty fizzy drinks cans rolling across the icy concrete. Abandoned cars, mostly with smashed windows.

No sign of life.

No sign of anything.

She decided to make a beeline for a card and gift shop at the bottom of the street. But the place was completely boarded up. It'd be hard to break into.

She walked further down. Saw an old record store. She knew Max liked his records. But they didn't have any record players or power back at the community, so that would be lost on him. But hey, maybe as a token gesture, it might be nice enough.

She stood there, lost. Felt like a real dick. She'd forgotten his birthday, and now she had no idea what to buy him.

She walked down the street, towards that record shop, when she noticed something.

In the window of this model shop, she saw a boat. A large boat model, like the one he'd made for her, only much bigger and more detailed. She knew he had this weird fascination with boats, and he'd made her a wooden one all that time ago, so really it was perfect.

She smiled. Looked for a brick on the road, then smashed the window, the sound echoing right the way down the empty street.

She reached in, being careful not to catch herself on any of the broken glass. Grabbed the boat, which was actually bigger and heavier than she first imagined.

She pulled it out of that gap in the window and stood there, smile on her face.

"You're better than Hailey's stupid fucking drawing," she said. Feeling a little guilty for it.

She went to turn around when she saw something in the middle of the street.

Or some*one*.

She got the strange feeling she wasn't alone.

CHAPTER SIX

Max wasn't sure how long he'd been walking after Aoife when he started to worry he'd lost her.

What the hell was she doing wandering off into the middle of nowhere, anyway? He'd followed her prints right down this country lane, and then they'd just stopped, in the middle of nowhere. Rex didn't seem to be having much more luck, either. Sniffing the ground, ears low. Uninterested.

Max sighed. Looked up ahead. He wondered what this was about. She'd gone storming off, out of the estate. Right after Hailey kissed him.

Could it be what he thought it was?

What he'd been denying for ages?

That there was undoubtedly something there between them, and she felt... what, jealous, maybe?

He shook his head. At the end of the day, they were friends. Good friends. And that's how things had to stay between them.

But what's so wrong with trying something else? Really?

He shook his head again. Better get rid of that damned thought fast. Not a road he wanted to be going down.

Speaking of roads... he knew he needed to stop fucking around here and actually get cracking on.

He walked further down this country lane. Still no signs of prints. Fuck, she wasn't much further ahead of him before. Where'd she got to?

He wanted to moan that this wasn't how he wanted to spend his birthday, but that was bullcrap. It was *exactly* how he wanted to spend his birthday.

Sure, he got on well with the people at the estate. He had friends there now, and he wasn't blindly pushing people away anymore.

But there was something about being alone, with Rex, in the great outdoors.

And there was something even better about it when Aoife was with him.

Damn it, Max. Stop being a sentimental old git.

Just find the girl and get her home.

Find her and enjoy your birthday.

He kept on walking further down this road. Beside him, he saw the woodlands emerging. Heard the wind against the trees. Made him feel a little uneasy. Those woods looked just like the one the whole charade with Christopher went on in six months ago. Seemed like forever ago.

He thought of how things concluded. How weird it all was. They hadn't had any problems with any of Christopher's people since Aoife and a few of the others had taken them away.

And sometimes, Max wondered.

He wondered exactly what'd happened.

But he never pushed Aoife for an answer. Never pried.

Even if it did keep him awake at night sometimes.

He went to follow the road off to the right when he noticed something.

There was an opening in the hedge on his left.

Someone had been through there.

He walked over to it, and he smiled.

There were footprints right across the field.

About the size of Aoife's.

"Well," Max said. "Looks like we're on her trail again, huh, Rex?"

Rex wagged his tail.

"Good dog. Good dog."

They climbed over the fence into the field. And as Max walked through it, he felt vulnerable. Exposed. And he couldn't shake that nagging feeling that someone was watching him.

"It'd be typical, wouldn't it, boy? For me to croak it on my birthday. Bloody typical."

Rex didn't seem interested. Just sniffed the ground. Stupid bugger.

Max followed these footsteps through the field. Followed them right through to a small town called Longridge. Nice little place. Real community feel to it. Didn't seem like anyone was here, either. Which was always a relief. Didn't want to run into any stragglers today. Although most outsiders were honest in their intentions, running into a rival group always brought its problems.

At the end of the day, supplies were scarce. So too was trust.

Better to just hunker down and keep within your own.

He walked down the hill towards the main stretch of Longridge. He'd lost track of Aoife now, but it wasn't a big place, so there'd definitely be a sign of her somewhere.

Abandoned cars stuck in the middle of the road.

Crows swooping down.

Shuttered up buildings and smashed glass.

But no sign of Aoife.

Max walked down the street. Everything was so quiet. He looked at every building, at every store. But no sign. Nothing.

"Aoife?" he called.

His voice echoed through the street. And he felt an idiot for shouting. If there was someone else here... then he didn't exactly want to draw attention to himself.

He looked around, and his heart started to pick up. He could feel it thumping away. There was no sign of her. Maybe she'd gone back. Maybe she'd not come down here. Maybe the footprints weren't hers at all.

He kept on going. Saw a rat scuttle across the street.

Saw movement up ahead. Movement that looked... well, not human, anyway. Probably dogs. Had to be careful with dogs.

He kept on walking through this empty street when he went past a library. The stench of something dead up on the slope, crows gathered around it.

"Doesn't look like she's here, boy," Max said. "Doesn't look..."

He stopped.

On the road, he saw something.

A boat.

A big model boat, right in the middle of the street.

On top of it, blood.

Fresh blood.

His stomach turned.

Aoife's blood?

The boat.

It all seemed too much of a coincidence.

Something had happened to her.

Something had...

He heard a growl. Rex.

"What is it, boy?"

When he looked around, he saw exactly what the issue was.

There was a pack of six mean and hungry-looking dogs.

And they were snarling and growling right at Max and Rex.

CHAPTER SEVEN

Max saw the pack of six dogs up the street and knew he was in deep shit.

They looked nasty. Snarling away. Hard to tell the breed too because they'd mostly lost their fur. Their ribs were on show. They looked hungry. Hungry and cold.

Max liked dogs. Rex had certainly converted him on that front. He never liked it when he ended up having to deal with them because at the end of the day, they were someone's pet, once upon a time.

But he had to detach from that shit now. Because they were nasty, and they were hungry, and they would go to any lengths to make sure they got what they wanted.

Just like people.

Rex snarled and growled. Which was the last thing Max wanted him to do now, much as he appreciated his loyalty. Any sign of aggression would only set this pack off.

Really, what Max needed to do was get the hell away from here.

Fast.

He lowered his eyes. Didn't want to look at these dogs directly.

And he held up a hand, too. Raised an arm to show he wasn't a threat. That he was just keeping his distance, minding his own business, and that he wasn't intruding on their space.

He could hear them barking. Growling.

See them moving towards him. Slowly.

"Come on," he muttered. "Just let me and my lad go. There's a dead dog up there on the slope. You lot go see to that."

But the dogs didn't seem to hear.

In fact, quite the opposite.

Three of them lunged forward.

Ran in Max and Rex's direction.

"Fuck," Max said. "No time to waste now, boy. We need to run."

He spun around. Ran. Rex by his side.

Behind, the rest of the dogs chased.

Predatory instincts kicking in.

Max looked around. They needed to get in somewhere the dogs couldn't get. He could grab his knife, use that on them. But he couldn't take all of them down. Maybe one or two, but six? No chance.

He looked over his shoulder.

Mean bastards nipping at his heels.

He didn't have long to find somewhere.

He looked around and saw a model shop on the left.

The window was smashed.

"In through there," he shouted.

He ran towards it. Clambered over the window, felt a nick on his palm. Broken glass. Fuck.

He climbed in there and turned around when he saw something that filled him with dread.

Rex was standing by the window.

Holding his ground.

Barking at these other dogs.

Protecting Max.

"Rex," Max said. "Come on!"

But Rex stood his ground.

Kicking back.

Hackles right up.

Six dogs surrounding him. All their attention on him, now. Not Max.

"Rex!"

But Rex didn't turn around.

He didn't even look at Max.

It was like he was giving him a chance.

A chance to get the hell through this shop to somewhere safe.

A chance to get away.

"Come on, boy," Max said. "I'm not losing you."

But then he saw the way Rex turned around.

He saw the way he looked into Max's eyes.

That loyalty.

There was no fear there.

There was only protectiveness.

That protective instinct.

He wanted to help Max.

He wanted to save him.

"Fuck," Max said. "Fuck."

He went to back away when he saw one of the dogs take a leap at Rex.

He heard Rex yelp.

And he knew he couldn't let this happen.

He tightened his grip around his knife.

Threw himself out of the window, grabbing a long shard of glass in the process.

He landed on the dog on top of Rex.

Disassociated himself from it.

Stabbed it right in the neck.

Felt the warm blood.

Heard the yelp and the cry.

And then he heard the frenzy getting louder.

Heard those barks.

Felt those teeth biting him.

But he was taking it.

He was taking it because he didn't want Rex taking it.

Rex was willing to die for him, so he was willing to die for Rex.

He swung his knife and the broken glass around waywardly. Blood splattering all over him. The taste of metal in the air.

Kept on swinging, kept on stabbing.

Kept on telling himself these weren't dogs.

These weren't people's pets.

They were just something in the way.

Something trying to attack him.

Something trying to hurt Rex.

Something doing him harm.

He kept swinging at them as he felt the bites on his body burning, stinging, when he noticed something.

They'd stopped.

There was just one left now.

It was one he hadn't noticed before. A little one. West Highland Terrier, by the looks of things. It had all its fur, some of which was splattered with the red blood of the other dogs. Reminded him of a movie he'd seen once. Game Night. Funny film.

He looked at this westie as it stood there. All around Max, the twitching bodies of dogs. All over the place, blood.

Rex by his side. Growling. Bleeding a little on his back where he'd been bitten, but not bad. Still okay.

He looked at this Westie and held his knife in hand.

Willing to do anything if it meant protecting Rex.

"Go on," Max said. "Walk away. This ain't your fight."

The westie stood there. Stubborn little mutt. Growling. Like it could still win this fight.

"You're outnumbered here. And I won't hold back. I promise I won't hold back."

He noticed something, then. This name tag on the dog's neck. Pebbles. Seemed vaguely familiar; he wasn't sure why. Maybe he'd known a guy with a dog called Pebbles once upon a time. Come to think of it ... it might've been a westie.

"Go on, Pebbles. Whatever kind of daft name is that anyway? Get your arse out of here. There'll be plenty more food for you."

But then something weird happened.

Pebbles lowered her ears.

Came walking up to Max.

And right up to Rex, too.

Wagging her little tail.

Max sighed. Rex sniffed her a bit, and she sniffed him. To be honest, Rex seemed keener on her than she was him.

But she was okay.

She'd learned her lesson.

Been put in her place.

Max looked around at the bloodied mass of twitching dogs.

Looked at the bites all over him.

And then he looked at the two dogs beside him, then at the empty streets of Longridge.

That's when the real problem hit him again.

There was no sign of Aoife.

She was gone.

And he had no idea where.

CHAPTER EIGHT

When Max got back to the estate, he had a thin slither of hope that Aoife might've just made her way back here and that he was on the wrong track all along. But there was no sign of her.

He stood by the gate. Rex was over in the kennels now, which he enjoyed, helping the new dog Pebbles settle in. She was actually quite sweet, truth be told. He tried to ignore the fact he was covered in the dried blood of the dogs he'd butchered on the road. At least the pair of them were alive.

"You're saying she just vanished?"

"I told you. I followed her prints to Longridge. But there's no sign of her there. No sign but her blood."

Geoff sighed. He was a bit of a miserable bastard, truth be told, but he was okay. The kind of bloke Max was used to running into back when he was a bouncer or in the police. Fat, bald, and always had a penchant for drinking far much more than he was capable of handling and causing trouble because of it.

But he'd softened these last few months. Kicked off every now and then when shit hit the fan. But when things were good, he was a decent bloke to have on side.

He stood there, hammer in hand. He'd been helping work on the east wall and didn't exactly seem best pleased that Max had dragged him down from it. "You know what Aoife's like. She's always wandering off."

"But not like this," Max said.

"And that's because you found her blood. And some boat. Right."

"Look," Max said. "I know how it sounds. The blood was fresh. And the boat... I think it's a birthday thing, maybe. I don't know."

"Max," Geoff said. "She's not a kid. She's gone walking off before. It's like I said. You know how she is."

"But not fucking like this, Geoff," Max snapped. "And not... not on my birthday."

Geoff's face dropped. He looked surprised by Max's outburst. He put down the hammer, walked a little closer to Max. "Look. If you're properly worried about her... we can get a small team and go out there. But truth be told we're pretty stretched here, and I'm not sure there's gonna be many volunteers to go searching for Aoife on a hunch if you don't mind me sayin'."

"I don't need many," Max said. "I don't need anybody. I was just hoping for a bit of support, that's all. But fuck it. I'll go myself."

"Go where?"

Max heard the voice from behind, and his stomach sank. Hailey.

"Hailey," he said. "It's... it's Aoife. She's gone missing."

He expected some jealous streak to show itself again, especially after before. But she looked genuinely concerned. "Gone... gone missing?"

"She went walking down towards Longridge. I got there, and I... I found some trace of her. But she's gone. No sign of her. I think something bad's happened."

Hailey walked up to him. Put a hand on his arm, then pulled it away, clearly not trying to be too forward. "Well, have you sorted out any search parties? Anything like that?"

Max looked at Geoff, who rolled his eyes, shrugged. "Look," Geoff said. "I like Aoife too. She's a good person. Gave me a right kick up the arse when I needed it six months ago. One I didn't know I needed. But I'm just saying, I think you're all overreacting a bit here. But if you want to go searching for her... Hell, be my guest."

Max sighed. He wasn't going to get Geoff on board. He got his hesitation, really. But he wished he could be less of a dick about all this.

"I'll come with you."

Max looked around.

Hailey.

"Hailey..."

"I know I haven't been outside much. I know I'm a farm girl. But I... I want to help."

"You don't know how to..."

"Look after myself? That what you're going to say?"

"I didn't mean it like that."

"Well, maybe I don't know the things you know. But I know one thing. I'm not letting you go wandering out there into something dangerous and risking your life on your own. I won't have it."

Wow. She was being really sweet about this. Which made Max feel even more of a dick about earlier.

"It's your birthday," Hailey said. "And the last thing you're going to be doing is going out there on your own."

"I appreciate that, Hailey. Really. But I can't—"

"You can. And you will. Question is, is Geoff here going to help us?"

Geoff looked at Max, then at Hailey, then back at Max again.

"Oh, whatever," he said, grabbing his hammer. "Got me with

that whole birthday emotional blackmail shit. What do you want, too? A fucking cake? Candles?"

"That would be appreciated," Max said.

"Come on then," Geoff said. "I'll have a word with a few of the lads. See if they'll join us. But trust me, mate. They ain't exactly gonna be queuing up to find her."

"Find who?"

The voice made Max jump.

When he turned around to the gate, he saw her, and he felt a whole wave of emotions.

Relief.

Anger.

The whole damned lot.

"Aoife?"

Aoife sauntered towards the entrance. She had blood on her arms. Looked like she'd been bitten. "Yeah?"

"Where the fuck have you been?"

"Whoah," she said. "I went to find a present for you. Ended up running into some vicious dogs. Might have to get these stitched up. But hey. Here you go. Happy birthday. It wasn't my first choice of gift, but I hope you like it."

She handed Max something in a small piece of red tissue paper, then walked past him, Hailey, and Geoff.

Geoff looked on. Raised his eyebrows. Opened his mouth.

"Don't," Max said. "Just don't."

CHAPTER NINE

"Hold still."

"It's hard to hold still when you're hurting me."

"And it'll hurt even more if you don't hold still."

"Max. Now really isn't the time for a fucking chicken and egg situation."

Aoife felt burning, stinging pain all the way down her left arm. It hurt like a bitch. To be honest, it hadn't even been that bad when the dog attack first happened. One of the little shits dug its teeth into her, and she had to kick it off and run for her life.

But now Max was seeing to it... yeah, amazingly, it felt a whole lot worse.

The stinging of the alcohol.

The pain of the stitches he'd woven through it with his remarkably steady hands.

The feeling of the warmth of his hands on her skin and how she strangely liked it...

No.

Don't even go there.

She looked up at him. He was so focused on her, on stitching her up. She could tell he was pissed with her. Wasn't saying as much, wasn't admitting as much, but she could just tell. He had that serious look to his face. Okay, he *always* had a fucking serious look to his face. But more serious than normal. And he was quieter than usual, too. Again, silence was something Max was clearly pretty comfortable with, but this felt different.

"So come on," Aoife said.

"What?"

"Get it over with."

"What're you talking about?'

"The lambasting. You've clearly got something on your mind. Why not just get to it?"

Max sighed. "Aoife... let's not."

"I'd rather you did than sulked like this. Go on. Have a nice birthday rant. It'll do you good."

"I almost died out there," Max said. "I... I almost died trying to find you."

"You didn't have to come find me. I was perfectly fine."

"You almost got yourself killed."

"Trust me," Aoife said. "You're being dramatic."

"Well, I almost died, and Rex almost died, too. I had to... I had to kill a bunch of dogs. Probably the same ones that attacked you. That didn't have to happen."

Aoife turned away. What sort of point was he trying to make, anyway? "I didn't ask you to come after me."

"Oh, don't start that business," Max said.

"But it's a fair point, right? Besides. I went out to get you a present. You like it, by the way?"

Max lowered his head, returned his focus to stitching Aoife's arm. "I... I haven't opened it yet. Wanted to open it when I got back."

He hadn't opened it? Really? Ungrateful bastard. He was quick to open Hailey's present. But hers could wait? Really?

She looked away. "Well, I hope you like it, whenever you get round to it."

"I saw the boat," Max said. "I'm guessing that was your Plan A present?"

"How did you guess?"

"I found it in the middle of the road. Your blood next to it."

Aoife sighed. "Those bastard dogs. It was perfect, too. You know, that westie you brought back here was the ringleader. You want to watch that one. Pebbles. Little Flintstones shit."

Max smirked. And Aoife felt like the weight in the air had lifted, now. Like the awkwardness between them had gone, thank God.

"Look," Aoife said. She could feel her heart pounding. It felt like this was the moment. The moment she'd been waiting for. The moment everything had been building towards. "I... I'm sorry I went wandering off like that. I guess I... I don't know why I did it. I suppose... Well. The truth is..."

She looked at Max. Felt that confession hanging in the air. Those words.

Tell him.

Just tell him the truth.

Tell him you love him.

Then she felt the fear kicking in, swallowing those words up.

"I'm guessing the truth is... I felt bad."

"Felt bad?" Max said. Almost like he wasn't expecting those words, either. Like he was expecting something else.

"I guess..." Aoife said. "I guess I felt bad because I l... Because I forgot to get you a present. And I suppose... I dunno. I just felt like I was a shit... a shit friend or whatever."

Fuck. She'd bottled it. Actually had that opportunity to tell Max how she felt, right there before her, and she'd bottled it.

Max was quiet for a moment, too. Like, it was seriously as if even he was expecting a bigger confession, too.

"And—and I guess I also wanted to say—"

A bang outside, from nowhere.

Aoife jumped.

Max turned around.

"The hell was that?" he said.

He got up. And Aoife got up, too, still a bit high on the adrenaline of everything. Of coming so close to telling Max the truth, then losing the moment, just like that.

"I don't know," Aoife said. "But it sounded..."

And then she heard another one.

And another.

There was no mistaking what they were.

Explosions.

And it sounded like they were coming from all around the community.

All around the estate.

She got up. Rushed outside, Max alongside her. Her arm still sore, but the last thing she could think about right now.

She could hear shouting.

Hear gunshots.

See people running through the streets.

And she could hear dogs barking, too.

And there was something else.

Something that filled her with terror.

Smoke.

Smoke at the east gate.

Then smoke at the other walls around the estate.

The explosions going off everywhere.

Inside.

Outside.

Everywhere.

And it was only when a woman called Sheila ran past, blood all over her face, that the reality of this situation sank in.

"We're under attack," she shouted. "We're—we're under attack!"

CHAPTER TEN

M ax heard the explosions and watched the smoke rising from every corner of this community, and he knew things were bad right away.

First, the screaming. Then, the sight of people running through the streets, covered in blood. The air growing hotter as flames started to climb the walls; as they rushed along the streets, far faster than seemed possible.

The sound of the dogs barking. Some of them yelping in fear.

And in the distance, the sight of blood.

Of dismembered limbs sitting in messy, fleshy puddles.

All over the place.

He looked around at all these horrors, and his first flashback was to war. To Afghanistan.

And then to that instinct, any army medic had.

The instinct to help.

But as he looked around, he saw the people on the ground here were mostly beyond helping.

Missing arms.

Missing legs.

And the explosions kept on happening.

Kept on thumping through the community.

"We're surrounded!"

Max heard that voice beside him. Saw it was Sam, one of the older blokes, well respected in this community. Known for his calm head. For his composed demeanour. For his rationality.

But right now, he looked shit-scared.

"Max."

Max looked around. Saw Aoife beside him. Saw her wide eyes. Her pale face. That fearful expression.

"We need to go," she said. "We—we need to get out of here."

"We can't just leave."

"The place is under attack, Max. It's... it's under attack. We can't just stay here. We have to go. We have to go, or we're not going to make it."

He heard Aoife's words, and he wanted to argue. Because she was wrong. There were people trapped here, and they needed saving. They needed *help*.

But then he heard the next explosion, or felt the heat growing more intense, or saw another flash of blood, and he knew deep down that time was running out.

"To the alleys on the west," he said. "There... there has to be a way."

He ran. Holding Aoife's hand. And as he ran, he found it so hard to keep going. Because he could see people lying on the streets. People covered in blood. People missing limbs. People crying out, gargling. Begging for help.

"I can't—"

"We have to leave, Max," Aoife said. Her voice was shaky, quivery. "I know... I know it's not easy. It's not easy for me, either. But we have to leave."

And Max heard her. Because the flames were getting hotter. The smoke was getting thicker.

And the more he moved through this street, the more he realised a horrible truth.

Time was running out.

He went to take a left, down the alleyways, when he saw something.

The kennels. The area where the kennels were.

Where Rex and the other dogs were.

He could see the dogs jumping at the metal fences. Some of them were dead. In pieces.

But some of them were still alive.

But that fence was still erect.

There was no way they were escaping.

They were going to burn alive if he didn't get in there and help them.

"The dogs," Max said.

"There's... Fuck. Rex."

"We can't leave him."

Aoife nodded, tears rolling down her face. "I don't... I don't know what else we can—"

"We can't just give up," Max said. "I... I can't just give up. I have to try, and you know it."

Aoife nodded. And Max felt bad for her. 'Cause in the urgency of the whole situation, he knew this was tearing her apart too. Rex was her dog before his, and she was making a very pragmatic and painful decision right now.

"You need to go," Max said.

Aoife frowned. "No. No."

"Don't make this about your guilt from the past," Max said. "Don't think of it like you're leaving me or like you're leaving Rex. Like you're running away. Save yourself right now. And I'll come back. I promise you, we'll both come back, okay?"

Aoife went to shake her head. He could see her wanting to argue. Wanting to fight.

And wanting to say something more.

"Go," Max said. "Go."

"You'd better come back," she said, tears streaming down her face. "And you'd better fucking bring my dog back with you."

"I will," Max said. "I promise."

She nodded. And then, as the chaos and the screaming continued to erupt around the place, Max watched as Aoife stepped away.

Eyes on him at all times.

He watched her reach the alleyway.

Watched her stop. Look back at him.

Watched her shake her head, then look away.

And then he turned around.

Turned towards the kennels.

He knew what he had to do.

He knew where he needed to—

A bang.

A bang right in the middle of the street, right between where he and Aoife were.

Flames erupting everywhere.

A building flattened.

And as he looked back, fear filling him, he knew that even if he wanted to go that way again, to find Aoife that way... his chance was gone.

There was only one way now.

He ran. Ran down the street. Ran towards the kennels. His ears rang. His nose was filled with smoke.

And the heat of the flames was growing hotter, hotter...

He ran over to the kennels, his focus on only one thing now—on getting Rex the hell out of those kennels. On getting all the dogs out of those kennels.

He reached the fencing and saw all the dogs jumping up at him. Pebbles was there. The other dogs were covered in blood.

But there were others lying down.

Pieces and chunks of others, all over the place.

He couldn't see Rex.

He yanked at the chains tied around the gate. Tried to pull it open, but it was stuck. Couldn't reach the main gate 'cause of the flames and the smoke.

And those flames were getting closer.

"Come on," he said. "Come on!"

He went to pull the gate again when he noticed something.

Rex.

Right at the back of the kennels.

Sitting down. Panting. Tongue out.

Like he was in shock.

Or suffering from smoke inhalation, he wasn't sure.

He pulled even harder at those gates, but they weren't coming loose.

They weren't going anywhere.

"Shit," he said. "Shit."

He looked at all these dogs, barking, yelping away, and then he looked at Rex, and he found himself having to make the hardest damned decision he'd ever made.

"I'm getting you out of there, lad. I'm getting you out of there."

He climbed over the fence.

Rushed over to Rex.

Picked him up.

"Come on, you big lump. Let's get you out of this mess."

He ran back to the fence. The rest of the dogs surrounding him. Wagging their tails. Jumping up at him like he was their saviour.

Even though he knew there was nothing he could do for all of them.

Even though he was only here for Rex.

He reached the fence. Went to throw Rex over the top of it. It wasn't a big drop, so he'd be fine.

But then he stopped.

The gate.

It might be flimsier from this side.

Flimsier from the weight of the dogs pushing against it.

He pushed against it. Hard. Harder than he had before.

And he saw the opening, narrow, but there.

Big enough for a few dogs to get out of.

"Go on," he shouted. "Go on!"

He watched as the dogs wormed their way out. As they ran away, through the street. Into the houses. Through gaps Max didn't even know were there.

And he didn't know the fate of them all.

He didn't know what happened to the bulk of them.

But he wanted to imagine they made it.

He wanted to imagine they'd be okay out there.

He watched the white westie, Pebbles, run off down the street.

Look back at him.

And he swore he saw gratitude in her eyes.

For giving her a second chance.

"Now for you," he said.

He pushed Rex through the gap. Hard, because he was too big for it.

And the flames were getting closer.

The smoke was getting closer.

Time was running out.

"Go on," he said. "For once in your bloody life, don't get lazy on me now."

He pushed Rex through. His back end sticking between the crack in the fence.

He went to give him one final push when he collapsed forward.

Rex was through.

He was out.

He went to climb over the fence to get out with him when he heard something.

A bang.

A huge bang, right behind him.

A hot burst of energy.

A rush of force as he flew forward, through the air.

And then he cracked against the ground and felt nothing.

CHAPTER ELEVEN

M ax opened his eyes.

His face was sore. He could taste blood. His body felt hot, on fire. He could hear something beside him. Like breathing. Panting.

He looked around. He could see something across the road. It looked like a body. Missing a head.

And then it hit him.

The explosions.

The attack on the community.

Saving Rex and the other dogs, and...

A nudge. A nudge on his left side.

He looked around and saw Rex beside him.

He was on his feet now, which was a big relief. Clearly not in a bad way like before. And by the looks of things, trying to get Max moving.

"Hey, lad. Hey. I'm coming. I'm..."

He looked around, and he saw the disarray.

He had no idea how long he'd been out, but clearly not long. The flames had totally swallowed the old dog kennels and were creeping closer to him and Rex. The street where he'd walked down, leading towards Aoife's escape route, was totally blocked and burning.

He hoped she was okay. Prayed she'd made it out alive.

Whatever the case, he needed to get the hell out of this community. And fast.

He went to stand. Felt sore all over, his knees especially. Looked all around. He could see dogs still running through the streets. A few survivors limping along, blood all over their faces, crying out. He wanted to help. Wanted to save as many people here as possible.

But he knew he didn't have time.

"Where are we gonna go, Rex? Where the hell are we gonna go?"

He looked around, trying to find the best way out, when he saw his house up ahead.

If he got there, he could go out the back window, climb over the fence at the back. It didn't look like anything had gone off over there. He was gonna be okay. He was gonna make it.

Both of them were gonna make it.

And if he didn't make it, well... at least he could get Rex out of here. That'd be enough for him. Knowing Rex was okay. Knowing Aoife was okay.

He ran. Ran through the streets with Rex by his side. Kept his head down now, resisting all instincts to help people, as goddamned hard as that was.

He kept on going down the street, navigating his way around the broken glass. The burning debris.

The entire estate looking like everywhere else in this world. Everywhere else abandoned. Like it had been battered.

Not looking like home anymore. Because it wasn't home anymore. This version of home was gone.

As had everyone in it, by the looks of things.

He reached the end of the street. Saw it was blocked. Shit. No choice now. Had to go through his house. Had to escape through the window. No other way.

He looked down the street and took a deep breath of the smoky air.

"Come on, lad," he said. "Through here."

He opened the door. Ran through the lounge. Couldn't be sentimental. Couldn't get bogged down in past attachments now.

Just had to get upstairs and get out of this place.

But as he went to climb the stairs, he noticed something.

It was on his living room table. Right in the middle of it.

The paper wrapping.

The gift Aoife had got him. The birthday gift.

The one he hadn't opened yet.

He rushed over to it, knowing he had no time to waste.

Grabbed it. Stuffed it in his pocket.

And then he ran up the stairs and to the window.

He could see to the gift later.

When he got out of this place, he could see to it.

He climbed the stairs.

Reached the back window in the bathroom.

Looked outside.

A sloped roof beneath him, which he could slide down.

Then just a jump out over the fence.

He could do this.

He could make it.

He could—

Another bang, close by.

So close that it knocked him back a bit.

He looked out.

Saw it was to the right.

Right by the fence he wanted to escape via.

Shit.

He had to do this, and he had to do this now. There was no more time to waste.

"Come on," he said. "Let's go."

He climbed through the window. Urged Rex to come with him, as resistant and reluctant as he seemed.

Sat on the sloped roof, watching as the flames spread across this stretch of the fence.

"Not much time left," Max said. "Got to get out of here. Now."

And then he slipped down the roof.

Fell to the concrete back yard with a smack.

But there was a problem.

Rex wasn't here with him.

He looked back and saw Rex still there, perched on the sloped roof.

"Come on," he said. "Now ain't the time to mess around, lad."

But Rex didn't seem to be budging.

"Rex!" Max shouted. "Get the hell here, right now."

Rex cowered back.

Max looked around.

The fence was burning.

The flames were picking up, getting closer.

"Don't do this to me," Max said. "Don't..."

And then it all happened so fast.

Rex jumped.

Jumped so far he slammed into Max, knocked him back to the ground.

Max fell back.

Felt something tumble out of his pocket.

That's when he saw it.

The piece of paper covering Aoife's gift.

Inside, a little metal model of an old motorbike, just like the one Max had ridden when the pair of them first met. The one he'd shot off on, then returned on to save her.

And beside it, a little pouch of Quaker Oats.

A note on the side of it.

"*I know you're precious about your porridge.*"

He smiled.

And then he noticed something else, right on the bottom of the note.

Three words.

"*I love you.*"

He saw those words, and time felt like it stopped. All of the chaos and destruction around felt like it faded into the background.

Because of those words.

Words he wanted to repeat to Aoife.

Words he wanted to say back to her.

Words he couldn't fight anymore.

He grabbed the motorbike. Grabbed the porridge pouch. Grabbed the note.

And then he pushed Rex from on top of him, and he faced the fence.

"Come on," he said. "It's now or never, boy. Now or never."

He looked at the fence.

Looked at the flames burning all along it.

Looked at them getting closer, almost swallowing up the opening.

"It's now or never," he said.

He held his breath.

Looked at Rex.

And then he closed his eyes, and he ran.

He felt the burning heat.

Felt the stifling pain, getting hotter and hotter.

Felt the smoke filling his lungs.

And then...

CHAPTER TWELVE

Aoife waited outside the gates of the estate and wondered where the fuck Max was and prayed to whatever god was up there that he was okay.

She'd heard another explosion right after she'd fled down the alleyway. She'd gone back. Tried to find her way through. She wanted to get to Max. Wanted to make sure he was okay. He was a fucking idiot for going back in there.

And she knew it was with good reason. She loved Rex more than anybody. And she dreaded to think of anything happening to him.

But then she knew at the same time that she had to survive. And Max had to survive. And it looked like there just wasn't enough time to save anybody.

She'd tortured herself for too many years for letting people down, for leaving them behind. For not doing more.

She was beyond that, now.

And still, the guilt hurt her.

She stood on the outside of the estate. The whole place was in ruin. Flames everywhere. Fire creeping up the walls of the community. Even the surrounding trees were on fire.

And the scariest thing?

There was no sign of the people who had done this.

No sign of why this had happened.

And the explosions. They got to Aoife. Because they seemed... controlled. They seemed organised.

They seemed planned.

Someone inside the community had to have been involved in this.

She stood there and stared and waited for Max to emerge—waited for *anybody* to emerge—but there wasn't a sign of life.

She wasn't sure how long she stood there. She wished she could actually *do* more.

But what the fuck could she do?

Her home was gone. Burning before her eyes.

The vast majority of her people were dead. Just like that, in an instant, dead.

She stood and stared at that alleyway and waited for Max to resurface.

Waited for him to appear.

She thought about the presents she'd got him. In a way, she was glad he hadn't found them now. Glad he hadn't found the note. She felt stupid about it. The "I love you"? Cringe.

He'd probably seen it anyway and felt too embarrassed about it to bring it up. Well, now at least he wouldn't see it. One twisted positive to come out of this.

She looked over at that blocked alleyway, waiting for a sign of life, losing hope, when she noticed something.

A few dogs. Running out of the community, out towards the woods.

That little Westie.

The one Max saved and brought back here, trotting off into the unknown.

That dog was in the kennels.

Just like Rex.

If these dogs had got out, then—

Another blast. Right over by the kennels.

Shit.

She didn't care anymore.

She had to go back there.

Max was in danger.

She ran. Ran over to the walls. But they were just too hot. She couldn't see any way in. Couldn't see any way through the flames. She was fucked. Completely and utterly fucked.

And so too was Max.

She worked her way along the wall. Just trying to find a way in. Trying to find a way through. Desperately, desperately searching.

But there was no way in.

There was no sign.

She backed away from the wall. Stared up at it. She didn't know what she was going to do. Didn't know where she was going to go.

Only that she couldn't leave here.

Not without knowing.

She backed off. Felt sick. Really fucking sick. The heat. The smoke. And everything that was happening. All catching up with her. All sending her mind spiralling. Racing.

"Please, Max," she said. "Please—"

"Aoife!"

Aoife turned around.

And when she turned, she saw him, and all the weight in her body lifted from her shoulders.

Max was there. Running towards her.

Rex by his side.

And he had something in his hand, too.

A smile on his face and something in his hand.

The motorbike.

The porridge oats.

And the note.

He looked at her with a smile on his face. He was covered in blood and black soot.

But he was here.

He was here, and he was alive.

"Max," she said. "Max..."

She went to run towards him, and she pictured the embrace already.

She pictured his big, warm arms around him.

She felt herself crying. Crying with happiness.

And she didn't even care how weak or how pathetic it made her look anymore.

Because he was alive.

Max was alive, and that was all she cared about.

She went to run towards him when she saw something.

Max's face, turning.

His eyes widening.

His smile dropping.

"Aoife—"

And then, out of nowhere, a gunshot.

A gunshot blasting through the air.

Max falling to the ground.

"Max!" Aoife shouted.

She went to run forward, but someone was on her.

Someone was holding her back.

She tried to break free. Tried to kick her way out.

"Max! Max!"

But Max was on the ground.

Lying there.

Clutching his chest.

Bleeding, badly.

He tried to drag himself towards her, but the blood was flowing out of him.

Rex was by his side. Barking.

And then running.

Running away.

And then as Aoife tried to kick herself free, tried to break her way out... she saw someone appear.

It was a woman.

She was very skinny. Lots of scars, all the way up her arms.

She was wearing a black face covering.

Only her eyes on show.

Bright green eyes.

She walked over to Max. Rifle in hand.

Stood over him as he tried to break free.

As he tried to drag himself forward.

"No!" Aoife screamed. "No!"

The woman stood over Max. Rifle pointed down at him.

And then she lowered the rifle.

Reached to her waist for a canister, poured the contents all over Max.

Then reached into her pocket and pulled out a lighter.

"No!" Aoife screamed. "Max! No!"

"Listen to his screams," the woman said. "Listen to his screams and remember. Remember."

She flicked the lighter.

Dropped it onto Max.

Silence.

A moment's pause.

A moment where time stood still.

And then his body burst into flames.

She heard his scream. Just for one second, she heard him scream, and saw him shaking, struggling.

She saw him look up at her.

His face disintegrating under the flames.

She saw him move his lips.

"I love you too. I love..."

And then she saw him go still as he disappeared under the mound of the flames.

"No!" she screamed. She didn't know where she was. She didn't know what was happening anymore.

She just wanted to get to Max.

"No!" she cried. Screamed. Falling to her knees, someone behind holding her close.

The woman walked over to her.

Looked down at her.

"We'll meet again," she said. Staring down at her with those green eyes. "When this has tortured you enough. I'm not ready for you to die yet. Not after everything you've done. Not yet."

But all Aoife could do was watch the flames rising from Max's prone body.

All she could do was watch the porridge oats and the note go up in flames.

All she could do was watch as Rex barked, ears back, and the rest of her community in flames behind her.

All she could do was watch.

And then she felt a heavy punch to her face, and darkness.

CHAPTER THIRTEEN

One moment, darkness.

The next moment, light.

Aoife was lying down somewhere. She couldn't tell where. Her head ached like a bitch. Her breathing felt difficult, laboured, like she had a nasty cold hanging over her. She'd had pneumonia as a kid, and this felt something like that. Wheezing. No matter how deep she tried to breathe, she could just never get enough air. Her chest felt tight, and her body felt shaky.

And yet, there was something hanging over her.

Like there was something she was ignoring.

Something she was failing to remember.

Something she didn't *want* to remember. Because it felt like remembering would be painful.

She opened her eyes just a little. It wasn't light like she'd been expecting. It was dark. The clouds were thick. Looked like a real fog was hanging over wherever she was.

She was outside. On the cold, freezing ground. Shaking.

Above, she could feel something falling. Cold, icy rain.

What was she doing out here on the ground?

Why wasn't she inside?

Had she passed out?

And her head. Her fucking head ached like mad.

Had she been attacked?

She looked around, saw the burned-out remains of the estate, and it suddenly hit her, all at once.

The attack.

The explosions.

And then...

She shook her head.

Closed her eyes.

The pain in her stomach so sharp that it felt like she was being stabbed.

She tried her best to push the memory away. Prayed she'd dreamt it. Prayed that it was some kind of nightmare.

But she couldn't hold the memories back.

And she couldn't deny just how real they'd felt.

How real they *were*.

Max.

Max, emerging from the burning estate, Rex by his side.

Then someone appearing out of nowhere.

Holding her back.

Someone shooting Max to the ground.

Max crawling towards her. Spluttering as that woman in the balaclava got closer.

As she poured petrol over him.

Aoife powerless to do anything to help.

Completely powerless.

She saw the way that woman lit the lighter.

The way she'd dropped it onto Max.

That moment's pause, where she thought he might fight free. Where she thought there might *still* be a chance.

And then the screams.

The screams and the struggling.

And then the silence.

All so quick.

But all so torturous.

She remembered the way the woman walked over to her, then. The way she looked at her with those bright green eyes.

Remembered exactly what she said.

"We'll meet again. When this has tortured you enough. I'm not ready for you to die yet. Not after everything you've done. Not yet."

And then the heavy punch to her head, and now...

She kept her eyes closed now. She could feel tears streaming down her cheeks. She was shaking. Freezing cold but boiling hot at the same time. Heart racing. Unsure if she could move a muscle. She just felt frozen. Frozen solid.

Because Max...

No.

He wasn't gone.

He couldn't be gone.

Not like this.

She didn't want to open her eyes. Didn't want to look and see; didn't want to find out the truth that she was clearly trying so hard to suppress.

For as long as she could dismiss it as a nightmare, she'd do that.

For as long as she could convince herself she was wrong about what had happened... that's what she had to do.

She'd hallucinated when she was heavily drinking in the past. Seen some really life-like things.

That was a possibility again, wasn't it?

Wasn't it?

But that feeling in her gut.

And that voice in her head.

No.

No, it isn't a possibility.

You saw what you saw, and he's gone.

She remembered dreaming, then. Dark dreams of dragging

herself across the grass. Towards the smoke. Rex barking at her to stop as she moved closer and closer to this mound. To this body. Blood on her hands.

And it was the blood on her hands in the dream that stood out most.

How she'd looked at that blood, and deep down, she'd had a feeling it meant something.

That there was a significance to it.

The way she'd dropped the lighter on Max.

Set him on fire...

No.

She couldn't think about it.

She couldn't go there.

She couldn't allow herself.

But as she lay there, she knew there was one option. Only one option here.

She certainly couldn't stay here all day. She couldn't just lie here.

She had to get up.

She had to *know*.

She gritted her teeth together and took a deep breath.

Then, she opened her eyes again.

Above, she could see it *was* actually still daytime. Cloudy. Rainy. Smoke floating above her, still catching on her breath, making her cough.

The flames still flickered away at the estate. She could smell burning. But there were no sounds of screaming anymore. No sounds of panic.

The calm after the storm.

Only not exactly. Because it felt ghostly. Haunted.

She turned over. Looked around. She was on her own. Completely on her own.

Only...

No.

There were bodies.

Bodies lying around her.

Bodies of people she recognised.

They looked like people who'd tried to escape.

All of them had bullet holes in their skulls.

Only she lived.

Why?

Why?

She turned over and looked ahead when she saw it.

The mound.

The burned mound of a body, right up ahead.

Right where he'd fallen.

Right where Max had fallen.

She didn't want to go over there. She didn't want to see.

But she had to.

She knew she had to.

She limped over there. Dizzy. Exhausted. Sore all over and broken inside.

The walk felt like it lasted forever.

Like she was trudging through tar.

Closer, closer, closer...

The closer she got, the more she expected him to look more familiar. For him to be more recognisable in some way.

But he just wasn't.

He was just a burned mess.

A burned mess. Charred. Blackened.

Holes where his eyes once were.

Teeth, on show.

The skin and the flesh all blackened, burned.

No hair left on his head.

She stood over him, and she looked down at him, and she wanted to cry. She wanted to cry, and she wanted to scream at him for going back in there.

She wanted to scream at herself for letting him.

And she wanted to tear off the face of the woman who'd done this.

Peel her skin away.

Gouge her fucking eyeballs out.

She stood there, over Max's body, and the one thing that wasn't burned sat there in the middle of this mess.

Sat there, between his blackened fingers.

The motorbike present she'd got him.

The little metal motorbike model.

She reached down. Throat wobbling. Unable to contain the emotion inside herself.

Picked up the motorbike model.

And as she did, she felt his burned fingers brush against hers.

The burned remains of the note there beside him.

I love you.

She went to take the motorbike away.

Went to take it away and get away from here.

And then she collapsed forward.

Collapsed onto his charred corpse.

And she cried.

CHAPTER FOURTEEN

A oife had no idea how long she lay there on Max's body.

The rain had stopped. The air felt cooler, but maybe that was just her. She was shaking. Couldn't stop shaking. Didn't even think she'd be able to move because her muscles were too weak. Could barely even think.

All she could think about was what had happened.

The way that woman shot him.

The way she'd burned him.

The way she'd burned everyone in her home.

She remembered the way she'd look at her, right in the eyes. And there was something in that look. Something... familiar.

No.

She couldn't think about that.

She couldn't even entertain that possibility.

Because if that were true...

No.

Don't go down that road, Aoife.

Don't you dare let yourself down that fucking rabbit hole.

She opened her eyes. It was dark. The flames had burned out.

Overhead, she could hear birds. Crows cawing. See some of them swooping down, feasting on the dead.

She thought about Rex, and she felt guilty right away. She'd barely even spared a thought for him since all this. She'd barely even spared a thought for *anything* or anyone since all this.

Just Max.

Just what had happened.

Just the anger and the pain and the rage she felt.

But she was going to have to get up eventually.

She was going to have to get up, and she was going to have to fight.

She felt something, then.

Out of nowhere, movement.

It came from her right.

From Max.

And even though she knew he was dead, even though she knew he was gone...

She turned around.

She saw something that made her feel ill.

A crow sat on top of Max. Pecking away at his burned flesh.

Looking at her like Max was nothing at all.

She felt rage inside her.

The little fucking bastard.

She lunged for it.

Grabbed it by its wings.

Pushed it to the ground and lifted her fists as he cawed back at her and tried to nip at her and fly away.

And then she let it go.

She let it go, and she shouted. Screamed. Buried her head into Max's body again. Let it all out. Cried.

She just wanted this to end.

She just wanted all this pain to end.

She let herself cry into Max's body, and she heard something behind.

Movement.

Definite movement.

She looked around. Everything looked hazy. Dreamlike.

And again, she found herself hoping that this *was* just a nightmare. A never-ending nightmare that she was just desperate to wake up from.

She wanted to wake up back at the estate. Back within the community.

She wanted to give Max his birthday present and watch him open it.

She wanted to tell him she loved him.

She wanted to spend Christmas and New Year with him.

But as she looked around, she saw something.

Movement.

Movement in the trees around her.

Right away, she felt this rage build up.

The woman.

The woman who'd killed him.

The woman who'd destroyed her community.

She might think she had the upper hand. She might think she could get away with this.

But she wouldn't.

She wouldn't fucking let her.

She got up. Tensed her fists. And without even thinking, she limped towards the trees, towards that movement.

"Hey," she said.

She reached into her pockets. Reached for any weapon she had on her. Found nothing.

So she looked around on the ground. Looked for something she could use. *Anything* she could use.

Saw a sharp shard of glass staring up at her.

She grabbed it.

Sliced her fingers a little in doing so.

Then she walked on.

Walked towards that movement in the trees.

"Hey!" she shouted. "I can see you. I can fucking see you. Come out, and let's finish this. Let's fucking finish this, right now."

She walked faster. Walked so fast that she broke into a jog, into a run.

She just wanted to get the pain out.

Wanted to get the anger out.

And there was only one way to do it.

To stab the fucker who did this.

To stab them and kill them and...

She reached the woods and saw the movement.

Saw someone emerge.

Immediately, her body softened.

"Rex," she said.

Rex stood there. Head lowered. Panting.

The poor dog could barely look at her.

He looked traumatised.

She dropped the glass to the ground and walked over to him. Welling up again. Just wanting to hug him. Just wanting to hold him. Just wanting to wrap her arms around him and feel his warmth.

But he backed away from her.

She stopped. Why would he do that? Why would he...

And then he barked at her.

Barked at her, then lowered his head again.

She stood there in the woods, shoulders slumping. She could see he was traumatised; see he was in a bad way.

But right now, she just wanted his comfort.

Right now, she just needed him.

"Rex," she said. "It's... it's me. It's Aoife. It's okay, lad. It's just me."

He looked up at her. For a moment, their eyes met.

And then he barked at her again, whimpered, lowered his

head, and turned away.

She stood there. Frozen. Totally still. It felt like she'd lost everything. In the space of however fucking long, she'd lost it all.

She didn't know what to do.

Didn't know where to go.

Didn't know a thing anymore.

But then she felt it.

Clearly.

She felt what she had to do.

She *knew* what she had to do.

The woman.

The woman with the mask.

The woman with the green eyes.

She had to track her down.

She had to find her.

She had to know.

She took a deep breath as she stood there, feeling exhausted, feeling weak, feeling completely broken down.

Feeling not with it at all.

Looked at Rex, who had his head slumped down to the ground.

"Come on," Aoife said. "There's... there's somewhere we need to go."

She went to turn around when she heard something behind her.

Movement.

And voices.

CHAPTER FIFTEEN

Aoife heard the voices behind her and felt that anger and that rage fill her body again.

Rex growled. Barked a little more, standing there before her. He wasn't barking at her now, though. He was barking at whoever was behind her.

She had visions of turning around. Of seeing that woman standing there. Black balaclava over her face. Bright green eyes piercing through.

And all the things she wanted to do with her, for what she'd done to Max.

All the ways she wanted to make her suffer.

All the ways she wanted to make her pay.

She turned around, wishing she was still holding on to that shard of glass, and she braced herself for anything.

When she looked around and saw who was standing there, it took her a few seconds to process it.

"Aoife?"

It was Hailey.

And for the first fucking time since knowing her, she didn't feel any resistance to Hailey.

She didn't feel like she hated her.

She was just so relieved to see her.

"Hailey," Aoife said.

And there was someone else here with her, too. Took her a second to realise who. But it was Geoff.

Geoff's face was covered in blood. His eyes were wide, and he looked traumatised. Glared at Aoife in a way he'd never looked at her before.

She saw Hailey, and she saw Geoff, and she was just so pleased to see them.

"Aoife..." Hailey started.

And Aoife didn't even think.

She just stepped forward.

Tumbled forward, right into Hailey's arms.

"It's okay," Hailey said. "It's—it's okay."

Holding her tight. Reluctantly, at first, but then tighter and tighter.

"Max," Aoife said.

"What about him?"

Oh fuck. She didn't know. She didn't fucking know.

"Aoife?" Hailey said. Moving her back a bit, so they were looking into each other's eyes now. "What... what happened to Max?"

The horror of the scene played out in her mind again.

Like it was happening all over again.

The gunshot.

The lighter.

The flames.

The screams.

She wanted to tell Hailey exactly what happened. Exactly what they'd done to him.

She wanted Hailey to feel her rage.

But in the end, she could only shake her head.

She could only cry.

And she knew Hailey would understand from that alone.

"Come here," Hailey said. "Come here."

She hugged Aoife for a long time. And Aoife was just grateful for the warmth. Just thankful to have someone here for her. And she felt bad. Bad for ever being such a dick with her. Bad for acting like such a jealous bitch.

Because Hailey was a good person.

She pulled away. Sniffed. Wiped her tears. Saw Hailey was crying, too.

"We barely got out ourselves," Hailey said. "We were by the community centre when the explosions started. Both of us got trapped under rubble. Geoff had his ankle stuck. Had to help him free. But we got away. Somehow... somehow, we got away. That's when they started shooting at us. Sam... he was with us. And they shot him. Shot him dead right beside us."

Aoife shook her head. She didn't know what to say. Didn't know what to think.

"We kept running," Hailey said. "Ran for our lives. I've no idea how we made it, but we did. We... we laid low for a while. Until we were sure they were gone. I don't know how many of them there were. I didn't see lots. But they... What happened here, Aoife. They must have planned this. Carefully. There's—there's no way this happened on a whim. There's nothing haphazard about it. But I just... I just don't understand. They haven't taken anything. They haven't even shown their faces. They just... they just did this, tried to kill everybody, then disappeared. And I just don't get it."

Aoife nodded. Didn't say anything.

But as she looked over Hailey's shoulder, she could see Geoff. See the way he was staring at her.

He hadn't said a single word yet.

And Aoife had a feeling she knew why.

"They wanted everyone dead," Hailey said. "But we made it. We... we survived. I'm not sure how many others did. We saw some dogs run by. But nobody else. If this is everybody... we have to be prepared for that. We need to—to find somewhere to shelter. For the night. Then go from there."

"They didn't want everyone dead," Aoife muttered.

"What?"

Aoife remembered the woman's words.

We'll meet again. When this has tortured you enough. I'm not ready for you to die yet. Not after everything you've done. Not yet.

And she thought about the fact she was alive at all.

The only one who wasn't alive by chance, but for a reason.

"Nothing," Aoife said.

And then she walked past Hailey. Walked past Geoff without saying a word.

"Aoife?" Hailey said.

"I need to find her."

"But—but we're in no position to go on the attack. We don't know who they are. Where they've gone. We don't know—"

"I don't give a fuck," Aoife spat. "I need to find her. I can't just let her go. Not after what she did."

"Aoife," Hailey said, walking towards her. "We need to stick together. It took us a long way to get here. We're all that's left. We can't just give up on each other. Not now."

Aoife felt bad. She felt sorry for Hailey. Because she agreed with her. The last thing the group needed right now was to collapse entirely, especially when by some miracle, there were people left.

But at the same time, she knew she had no other choice here.

"I get it. And I'm sorry. But I can't... I can't just let her go. Not after all she did."

She looked at Hailey, then at Geoff, who was still quiet.

Geoff staring at her like he had something on his chest but was suppressing it. Something uncharacteristic for him.

"I have to find her. And I'll make her pay. For what she…"

She stopped speaking.

Because she heard something.

Voices.

Voices, in the woods, nearby.

And then, out of nowhere, a gunshot.

CHAPTER SIXTEEN

The second Aoife heard the gunshot, she didn't feel afraid.

She just wanted to get the fuck to the source of it so she could get hunting the bastards who'd killed Max—and destroyed her community.

Hailey and Geoff both looked around, over towards where that gunshot came from. Rex backed off again, whining, clearly still traumatised by everything. It was just the one gunshot, still echoing through the silence. And it sounded a fair way away, too.

But Aoife didn't give a damn.

It had to be the people who'd attacked her community.

It had to be the people who'd killed Max.

She didn't hesitate.

She ran.

Ran towards the trees.

"Aoife!" Hailey called.

And as much as she wanted to apologise, as much as she wanted to hold back, Aoife didn't listen to her.

She had her own shit to deal with now.

She ran through the trees, leaving Hailey, Geoff—and even Rex behind. She felt guilty about that. Didn't want to leave Rex. He meant so much to her. Meant goddamned *everything* to her.

But this was more important.

He was okay with Geoff and Hailey. They'd look after him.

Okay, Hailey wasn't exactly the most qualified. But Geoff knew how to fight.

She ran further through the trees, further into the darkness. She couldn't hear gunshots, but she could hear voices now. Sounded like talking. Laughter.

She kept on going when suddenly she saw movement up ahead.

She stopped.

Dropped to the ground, in a tall patch of grass, right between some trees.

She could see four people, men, walking through the woods. One of them was holding a pistol.

"You shouldn't go firing that thing in the middle of the night, Kent," one of them said. "Only gonna draw attention to us."

"Stop being such a whiner. You're worse than my bloody wife."

Aoife watched these people walk by, and she knew who they were. Looters. Scavengers. The kind they'd fought off a few times over the last few months. Low lives. Didn't really have any sort of plan, just went from place to place, stealing whatever they could to survive off. Vultures.

No doubt heading to the burning remains of the estate to find out what they could grab for themselves.

She felt disappointed. Because they weren't who she'd wanted to run into.

They weren't the woman or her people. They couldn't be. They weren't nearly elaborate enough to pull a trick like that at the estate.

Nowhere near as organised.

But they were dangerous. Scavengers had been known to kidnap people before. Women in particular were top targets, and kids, for reasons that didn't need explaining.

So as much as Aoife wanted to deal with them—as much as she wanted to take her anger out on them—she knew she'd be better off getting away from here right now.

She turned around slowly when she heard another voice.

And his words caught her attention.

"That group over in Morecambe," he said. "You're gonna need to learn how to use a gun if we're gonna break into their place."

"Break into their place? You actually think there's a chance of that?"

"As long as I'm alive, I'll not give up on that. Especially since we know they're out here now. God only knows what drove 'em to blow this place up within an inch of its life. If there's even any life left there at all. Now come on. Get a fucking move on. Ain't got all night."

Aoife heard the people walk off through the woods. And it was those words that stuck with her. About Morecambe. About the explosives.

Could they be the people?

She heard them walking off towards her old home, and every instinct in her body told her to drop back. Because she was on her own, and she didn't have any weapons. And there were at least four of them—possibly more out here in the woods. Probably a whole host of scavengers out here, ready to loot the shit out of the place.

But another part of her didn't give a damn.

She wanted to know more about who she was dealing with.

She wanted to know more, and she wanted to fucking rip off the faces of anyone who got in her way.

She stood up. Saw those men moving forward. Tightened her fists.

And then she went to step forward.

That's when she felt the hand around her mouth.

The arm around her throat.

"Ssh."

CHAPTER SEVENTEEN

Aoife felt the arm around her throat, the hand covering her mouth, and she knew she was in deep shit.

She tried to break free. Tried to swing her fists at whoever the hell was holding on to her, as in the distance, those scavengers got closer to the estate.

"Be quiet, Aoife. Be quiet. It's me. Come on. There's nothing for us here."

Wait. He knew her name? And his voice...

Fuck. It was Geoff.

She tried even harder to break free of his grip, to speak. Wanted the bastard to let go of her, pronto.

"Come on," he said, trying to drag her back into the trees. "Don't know what the hell you think you're doing. Gonna get yourself killed. And the rest of us killed if you ain't careful. And I ain't keen on dying after barely surviving today."

Aoife tried to dig her heels in, but it was useless. Geoff was way stronger than her. And as much as she wanted to go after those scavengers, as much as she wanted to find out about Morecambe, where they spoke of a group with explosives... she couldn't budge.

"Let's get you away from here. Let's both get the hell away from here. Before they..."

She didn't know why he stopped. Not at first.

But then she heard the footsteps in the woods behind her.

Coming their way.

"Shit," Geoff said.

There was someone coming.

There was someone *frigging* coming.

"Get down," Geoff said, dragging her to the ground. "Hailey... She's on her own out there with Rex. You'd better be quiet. If not for me, then for her. And for your damned dog, understand?"

Aoife saw the way Geoff glared at her, listened to those footsteps crunching across the frosty ground, getting closer.

And as much as she wanted to go after the scavengers and find out what they were talking about, she nodded.

"Good," Geoff said. "You'd better."

He moved his hand away, and Aoife gasped for air as the pair of them lay there on the forest floor.

"Could you do that a bit quieter, maybe?" Geoff asked.

"Oh, I'm sorry," Aoife wheezed. "I'll try my best to be quiet for you after you've just frigging strangled me."

"That'd be appreciated."

She shook her head. Looked around into the darkness of the woods. Over towards those footsteps. She didn't know who they belonged to. Had to assume more scavengers.

But this group.

The one from Morecambe.

The one who had to be responsible, somehow.

They couldn't be far away, right?

They couldn't have just left her here. Especially when that woman said she had a bone to pick with her.

When she said she wanted her to suffer.

She squinted into the darkness, into the trees, when she saw a figure appear.

It was hard to make out at first. Just a dark silhouette, standing there amidst the trees.

But then, as Aoife squinted, as the moonlight peeked through the branches, she noticed something that made her skin crawl.

It was a woman.

Dressed all in black.

Wearing a balaclava over her head.

Aoife felt cold.

She lost all sense of her surroundings.

All sense of everything.

All that mattered to her?

This was the woman who'd killed Max.

This was the woman who'd destroyed her community.

She was right here.

"Just stay low," Geoff whispered. "Stay low, and she won't... hey!"

Aoife didn't process a thing.

She ran.

Ran as fast as she fucking could at the woman.

Didn't care that she didn't have a weapon.

Didn't care about anything.

She just wanted to kick the shit out of her for what she'd done.

Torture her.

Murder her.

The woman didn't see her at first.

Then she turned. Very suddenly.

Looked right at Aoife with those green eyes again.

And Aoife half-expected her to stand up. Half-expected her to fight.

But instead, she turned, and she ran.

Aoife launched herself after her. She had to track her down. Had to chase her. Had to kill the bitch.

And then she felt something around her ankle.

Something wrapped around it. Sent her flying to the ground. The woman disappeared into the trees.

"I told you," Geoff said. "I told you to stay the hell quiet."

It was only when Aoife looked around that she realised it was Geoff who stopped her.

"Let me go!"

"I'm not letting you go anywhere."

"The woman. The woman who fucking killed Max. She was there. She—she was there and—"

"I don't give a shit if the Devil himself is there right now. What I care about is surviving. And... Awh, crap."

Aoife heard voices. Saw the scavengers pointing back at the woods, shouting, running their way.

"See what you've gone and done now?" Geoff said.

But Aoife wasn't with it.

Her only focus was that darkness in the woods, where the woman had disappeared to.

"Come on," Geoff said. "If you don't frigging come back with me now, I'll leave you here. I swear I'll leave you here. But good luck with the scavengers. They look like a friendly fucking bunch."

Aoife wanted to take her chances. She was seething. Seething that Geoff had stopped her. That the woman had got away.

But when she looked around and saw the scavengers coming towards her, she knew that even though she wanted to find out about Morecambe—find out about this woman—there was no hope in standing against them. She'd only get herself in deeper shit.

And she needed to live right now. If only to murder the bitch who'd killed Max.

"Come on," Geoff said. "Get up. Let's go."

She looked back at that darkness. Into the woods, where the woman disappeared.

And then she shook her head, sighed, and followed Geoff off into the woods, away from the scavengers, into the darkness.

CHAPTER EIGHTEEN

Aoife stood in Max's old bedroom and felt the emptiness hanging in the air.

It was strange, being back here, at his cottage in the woods. Dark. Dusty. A musty, un-lived smell to the air. Everywhere was echoey. Like it was clear already that nobody had been here for a long time. Lifeless. Soulless.

Like the house itself knew that its old owner was gone.

She looked at his bed, still unmade from the last time he'd slept in it, a year ago. Looked at the bare walls. The watch on the cabinet at the side, the time stopped right at midnight. She looked at the clothes in the wardrobe. Went over to them. Smelled them. That sweetness of his skin, making her feel like he was still here.

But the reminder, the sinking feeling in his stomach, that he was gone.

She saw the photograph, then. Right on the bedside cabinet. Max. His wife, Kathryn. And his son, David.

Saw them there, smiling. Happy.

And it pained her to admit she barely recognised him in this photo. For even as much as he'd rediscovered his love of life over the last few months, there was still a haunted expression to his face. Like a spectre was hanging over him at all times.

In this photo, he looked happy. He looked alive. He looked in love.

She smiled, welling up. Put the photo back down.

Then she heard footsteps by the door.

She sighed. "You should learn to sneak up on people better."

"I'd say I did a pretty decent job in the woods, wouldn't you?"

She turned. Saw Geoff standing there, leaning on the door. Not quite looking into her eyes like he was trying to avoid all contact.

"You shouldn't have stopped me out there."

"I did it for your own sake, and you know it."

"That woman," Aoife said. "She killed Max. She shouldn't have got away—"

"You went running towards her with no weapon. No nothing. Scavengers lurking nearby. You coulda killed yourself. You coulda killed all of us. Really, I did you a favour."

Aoife sighed. "I appreciate it, I guess."

"I'll take that as a thanks. You should get some rest, anyway. It's late."

Aoife nodded. She felt knackered. But there was no way she was sleeping tonight. She wasn't sleeping until she found that woman.

Until she tortured her and destroyed her for what she'd done.

"So should you," Aoife said.

Geoff laughed a little. "Oh, I'm a night owl. Always have been. Got by on three hours sleep a night back when I was a lorry driver. You kind of learn to grab what you can when you do summat like that."

"Hailey okay?"

"Flat out. Think it's hit her hard, though. The shock. Like... she's a good woman. Nice. But she's not as hardened as us two, y'know. Kind of sheltered. From the bad stuff. From the... the dark stuff."

He looked at Aoife, then. And she felt a twinge of sickness in her stomach. Was he suggesting something?

Implying something without saying as much?

"Anyway," Geoff said. "Tomorrow's... tomorrow's a new day. We figure out where we're going from there. At least we're—"

"I know what I'm doing tomorrow. I'm going to find that woman. I'm going to go to Morecambe, and I'm going to find out more about the group who did this. And I'm going to make them pay. For what they did to us."

Geoff opened his mouth like he was going to argue. Then he closed it. Sighed. "All in a day's work, huh?"

"I don't care how long it takes. I'm not resting until I've brought them to justice."

"Don't doubt you for one second."

He looked down again at the floor. A silence between them.

"Aoife," he said. "You don't think this might be to do with—"

"No," Aoife said.

Even though she felt it.

Even though she feared it herself.

But she couldn't face that.

She couldn't face up to the possibility that it might be to do with what she feared it was.

What Geoff clearly feared it was.

Because that would mean it was on her.

And she couldn't bear to carry that sort of weight.

He looked like he was going to say something else.

Then, he just nodded. Half-smiled.

"Try to get some sleep," he said. "Big day ahead of us tomorrow. Tough day. First day of our new world. It ain't gonna be easy. So be ready."

Aoife nodded. "You, too."

He stood there a few seconds. Like he was going to say something else. Almost like he was keeping something from her. And it felt... creepy, somehow.

And then he just turned around.

Walked away.

Left Aoife alone in the darkness, alone in Max's old bedroom.

The guilt creeping through her system.

The thoughts of shame filling her mind.

No.

It couldn't be what Geoff said.

It couldn't be because of that.

But she kept on seeing those green eyes, staring back at her...

She kept on seeing them, and as much as she tried to push back, as much as she tried to fight against them...

She couldn't.

CHAPTER NINETEEN

G race lay on the forest floor in the middle of the darkness.

It was pitch black, and it was cold. She couldn't stop shivering. Not just with the cold. But with what she'd done, too. With everything that'd happened today.

The explosions.

The killings.

And... her.

She swallowed a lump in her throat. It'd been a crazy day. And a whole host of emotions ran through her body. Partly relief. Partly pride.

But also shame, too.

Shame and fear.

It wasn't the cathartic release she was hoping for.

But that would come.

She knew, in time, that would come.

She stood up. Squinted through the darkness of the forest, over at the estate. Things couldn't have gone better. Stealing the explosives from the group over at Morecambe. Bribing one of the estate community to lay them down, get them ready to blow.

And then...

The man.

The man staggering out of the walls of the community towards her.

The smile on her face as she saw him.

A smile of love.

And at that moment, at that instant, Grace felt it all over again.

The love *she'd* felt for her sister.

And how it'd been taken from her.

She'd lifted her rifle and shot him.

Then she'd gone over to him.

Burned him while her little mole held the girl back.

Listened to him squeal.

Watched the girl cry. Scream. Hysterical.

And she'd felt bad, letting that man burn. Making him suffer like that. It didn't feel like something she wanted to do at all. She wasn't a monster. She was a good person. Someone who had always done things by the book.

But she'd never experienced loss like she'd experienced it six months ago.

She'd never felt the urge for revenge like she'd felt it this last half-year.

And she'd never lived in a world where it was so easy to get that revenge without facing any consequences.

But right now, standing here in the dark, there was an emptiness.

A feeling that she'd never scratch the itch for revenge.

That she'd never fill the hole of loss that had opened in her life.

That even if she made the woman suffer in ways she felt bad even imagining, it wouldn't be enough.

She took a deep breath.

Thought of that woman.

Felt the hatred for her.

And she felt all the pain she was going to cause her, and it fuelled her.

Charged her.

It was only just beginning.

She went to turn around and walk away when she heard footsteps behind her, approaching through the trees.

She lifted her pistol for a second, when she saw it was him.

He stepped out of the trees.

Walked up to her.

Stern look on his face.

She lowered her pistol. "You."

"One way to say 'thanks'," the man said. "Now. About payment."

"You'll be paid when it's done."

"Done? You destroyed my community. Killed every damned person in there. And I've got her here for you, right on a plate. We not done yet?"

Grace walked up to the man. Pointed the pistol, right at his chest. "Don't forget the fact I'm keeping you alive at all is a favour in itself. After what you were a part of."

The man lowered his head. Nodded. "Right."

"So you're still in?"

"What?"

"You'll help me. With the next step."

The man opened his mouth like he was going to protest. Then he sighed. "I guess I don't have a choice."

Grace smiled. Pulled the pistol away. "Good. Then this is what you have to do."

CHAPTER TWENTY

Aoife gasped and jolted upright.

It was light. Flames. Flames surrounding her. Getting closer to her.

Max, lying there.

Burning.

Screaming...

Then she realised something.

She wasn't surrounded by flames at all.

She was lying on Max's bed at his cottage in the woods. She felt groggy, mouth dry, head aching. Must've fallen to sleep. The curtains were open, and bright winter sun shone right in. On the branches of the trees outside, she could see a pair of robins, both chirping away.

She got up, a little dizzy. Saw Rex lying at the foot of the bed, wagging his tail a bit. Seemed to have perked up a bit since outright rejecting her yesterday. But still wasn't quite there.

She knew she'd have to be patient with him. Give him time.

She squeezed the bridge of her nose, a sense of urgency suddenly kicking in as she stood and walked across the wooden floorboards of the bedroom. She had no idea how long she'd slept. Her sleep must've been deep and dreamless, something she was thankful for. Wasn't ready to handle the nightmares. Not now. Not ever.

She walked to the bedroom door and heard Rex whine a little.

She turned around. Saw him still lying there. Still not making eye contact with her. Damn. Poor sod. He wasn't usually like this.

She walked over to him. Slowly. Crouched right beside him. Stroked his fur, right down his head and his back.

"I know, pal. I know. I miss... I miss him too."

And then he did something that made her feel a lot better.

He nuzzled his head right into her thigh.

She welled up a little when he did that. Smiled. That's all she'd wanted, really. Some reassurance. Some show of affection. She'd appreciated it from Hailey yesterday. It felt... weirdly comforting.

But from someone as close as Rex, yeah, that made a difference.

"I'm glad you don't hate me," she said.

Maybe he should. Because this is on you.

"No," she muttered. "No."

She got up. Walked out the room. It was quiet in the house. So quiet that it felt unoccupied. Like nobody was here at all.

She remembered Geoff and Hailey coming back here with her, so maybe they were just asleep still. Or maybe they'd gone out and left her to sleep.

She hoped they were okay, wherever they were.

She climbed down the creaky stairs, Rex by her side.

Walked past the front door.

Walked towards the kitchen table.

That's when she saw it.

Almost missed it at first. But it was there, on the floor, right by the door.

A note.

She went cold and numb right away.

A shiver crept down her spine.

That folded piece of paper.

A little speck of blood, right on the corner.

She walked over to it slowly. Not wanting to see its contents. Not really.

She reached down.

Picked it up.

Please be a coincidence. Please be something I just missed before.

She opened the note.

And when she read what it said on there, her entire body went numb.

When she read it, she threw it to the floor.

Her heart racing.

Breathing difficult.

Because those words.

Those words were confirmation of what she'd been trying to hide from.

What she'd been trying to run from.

What she'd been trying to avoid all along.

But now couldn't.

She turned around. Walked into the kitchen area, grabbed her shoes. Then she went down into the cellar, packed a rucksack with food supplies.

With a knife.

And grabbed one of Max's old hunting rifles.

She walked over to the door. Stood there. Shaking.

Those words replaying, again and again.

Taunting her.

There was no way she could deny what this was about anymore.

There was no way she could hide from it.

She looked down at the floor, at the note, and saw those words staring up at her once again.

. . .

I'VE TAKEN *them to where this all started.*
   You know where to go.
   Face your crimes.
   —Grace.

CHAPTER TWENTY-ONE

A oife saw the warehouse in the distance and felt really fucking sick.

It was a long time since she'd been here. Six months ago. She'd never had any intentions of coming back here. Wanted to keep this place firmly in the past.

But that note.

The note left at the door to Max's cottage by a woman called Grace.

I'VE TAKEN them to where this all started.
You know where to go.
Face your crimes.

SHE KEPT on replaying those words, again and again.

Where this all started.

She remembered the look in that woman's eyes behind the balaclava. Those bright green eyes. She wanted to believe she'd got it wrong. Wanted to convince herself that it was all in her head.

Because what she feared was impossible.

Nobody could have survived what had happened.

Nobody could have survived what she'd done.

You know where to go.

She looked at the warehouse. It was bright. Middle of the afternoon. It'd taken her a while to get here. A good few hours. This place was out of the way. Well out of the way.

There were things that didn't add up. If this was about what she feared it was about, then why take all this time to strike back? Why take six months?

Then she thought of Max.

Thought of him stepping out of the estate, smile on his face. Clearly so happy to see her.

Thought of him walking towards her.

Then the gunshot, piercing his chest.

Dragging himself along the ground, bleeding out.

The woman—Grace—walking over to him.

Pouring that gasoline over him.

Then dropping the lighter on him...

Aoife felt herself tensing up. Losing herself in the hatred again.

She didn't give a shit who this woman was. She didn't give a shit if she *was* who she feared she was, as much as she couldn't see how that was possible.

She'd murdered Max.

She'd killed so many of her people.

And she'd destroyed her home.

She was going to pay for what she'd done.

Face your crimes.

That bitch had no right saying *anything* like that if she was who she thought she was.

Face *her* crimes?

Get a fucking grip on reality.

She walked slowly towards the warehouse. Rex close by her side. She didn't want to let him out of her sight. The warehouse seemed quiet. Abandoned. Empty.

But she felt like someone was watching.

Hell. She knew damned well someone was watching.

She thought about Hailey. Thought about Geoff. And she thought about what Grace said to her too, about torturing her. About her not being ready to kill Aoife yet.

She hoped Hailey and Geoff were okay.

But she didn't hold out much hope.

She got closer to the warehouse. She could feel her heartbeat pounding in her skull. She'd never intended coming back here when she'd left the last time. No reason to.

Besides. She didn't want to remind herself of what she'd done that day.

Didn't want to remember.

She reached the door to the warehouse and stopped.

Took a deep breath.

Then, she opened the door.

She could still smell smoke in the air. Burning, catching in her nostrils. A reminder of what'd happened. A reminder of Max, too.

It made sense. In a horrible, fucked up way, she'd been in denial. Because the method. The way she'd done it. The way she'd killed him.

It added up.

It all added up.

She stepped inside the warehouse. Her footsteps echoing against the cold metal of the floor. If her heart started beating any faster, it might just burst out of her chest.

She could see something in the middle of the warehouse.

Didn't want to look at it.

Didn't want to see it.

Didn't want to remember.

She walked around it. Up some steps, up to a platform. The same place she'd stood that day six months ago.

The place she'd held the match.

The place she'd dropped it from.

She walked towards the end of the platform. Still not wanting to look. Not wanting to see.

But knowing she had no choice.

She stood there. Held her breath.

Then, she looked.

On the floor, right in the middle of the warehouse, she could see a circle.

A circle just like the one she'd created all those months ago.

In the middle of it, she could see bones.

Skeletons, staring up at her.

She felt sick. They were still here, just like she'd left them. And even though they were just bones now, she swore she could see terror in their eye sockets. Pain on their faces.

She heard a footstep behind her.

Heard the floor creak.

When she turned around, she saw someone standing there.

The woman.

The woman with the balaclava.

Green eyes staring right at Aoife.

Rifle in hand.

Pointed at her.

"I knew you'd come."

CHAPTER TWENTY-TWO

The second Aoife saw the woman—Grace—standing there at the opposite side of the platform, rifle in hand, she lost all sense of her surroundings.

"You," she said.

Grace stood there. Black balaclava over her face. Those piercing green eyes staring at her from behind it. Rifle in her hands pointed right at her.

"Didn't take you long to figure out where I'd be," Grace said.

Aoife walked towards her without even thinking.

"Not another step," Grace said. Lifting her rifle.

But Aoife didn't hear her.

She just kept walking towards her.

A bang.

A bang, right at her feet, stopping her in her tracks.

The blast from the rifle.

"I warned you," Grace said. "Not another step."

"I don't give a fuck about your rules, you murdering bitch."

"You have a nerve saying that after what you did to my people."

"Your people? The fucking cannibal cult, you mean?"

"You really think we were all on board with that?" Grace shouted. "You really think we *wanted* that? That we didn't want to break free just as much as you did? Do you really think there weren't things going on behind the scenes? You saw it yourself. My people. They... they stood up for your people. They *died* for your people in the end. And how do you thank us? By leading us like cattle to slaughter."

"Like you did to—"

"I didn't do a fucking *thing*. I found a home for me and my sister. I tried to survive the best life I possibly could knowing full well what was going on wasn't good. I felt guilty about it, every single day. And when we finally got a second chance—when we were finally free—you set us on fire. You burned us. You took that chance from us."

Aoife tasted sick in her mouth. She didn't want to hear the genuine sadness in this woman's voice. Didn't want to acknowledge that through all her twisted logic, she might actually have a point.

She thought this.

Then she remembered Max.

"You didn't give Max a chance," Aoife said. "He... he was a good man. And you killed him. You burned him. You burned so many people."

The woman lowered her head just a little. "I know you won't believe me when I say I'm sorry. But I am. I really am."

"Bullshit. I'm really supposed to believe that crap after what I saw you do?"

"You looked me in the eyes when you dropped the match," Grace shouted. "You looked me in the eyes, and you saw me begging. You saw me crying. You looked me in the eyes as my people all died around me, and you had a chance. As my sister burned to death right next to me, begging for my help. You had a chance to try something. Anything. But instead... you just turned away."

Aoife saw Grace walking towards her, then. Rifle still raised. Pointed.

Saw her step further into the light.

Rex growling by Aoife's side.

"And now I have to live with it. Not just the memories. Not just the nightmares, every single night, which were already bad enough after everything I was forced to do under Christopher's rule. But the scars. The actual, physical scars. I can't even look at myself anymore. I can't even let anyone else look at me. Because... because I'm ashamed. I'm ashamed of what I am. And that's because of you."

She stood there. Rifle pointed. And Aoife wanted to throw herself at her. Any second she got close to feeling any kind of pity, she remembered Max. Screaming. Then burning.

The smell of his burning body sticking in her nostrils.

"So what now?" Aoife said.

"What now?" Grace said. "That's all you have to say? What now?"

"You have Geoff. You have Hailey. They're my people. I won't beg. But they don't deserve whatever you're planning on putting them through. If you have to put anyone through anything... it's me."

Grace looked at her through that balaclava. Her green eyes darting from side to side.

"I want to let them go. Really, I do. But then... then I think of what you did, and I think about how you did it, and I want to hurt you. I want to hurt you so, so deeply. Do you know my sister was right there with me when it ended? That when my blindfold melted away, I had to watch her burn, too? She didn't want any of what Christopher was doing. We just... we just went along with it because it was the safest option. And it was hard to get away. Hard to be a deserter. We weren't proud of it, but we did what we had to do to survive, and we hoped Christopher would get his comeuppance one day. I watched her scream. I watched her eyeballs burst in the heat. I watched her burn right before my eyes. And there was nothing I could do but escape. Climb on the burning bodies and escape."

Aoife lowered her head. She felt a bit dizzy. A bit sick. "Where are Geoff and Hailey? And where are the rest of your people?"

"The rest of my people?"

"Someone held me back. When you killed Max, someone held me back."

Grace laughed, then. And it was the first time Aoife had heard her laugh. "I don't have any people. You took all my people away from me."

That didn't add up. The shit about the people in More-cambe. And then the person holding her back when she watched what happened with Max. "Then who... who held me back?"

Grace sighed. "I want to show you something. Come on."

She turned around, and Aoife saw her window of opportunity.

She saw her chance.

A chance to get to her.

A chance to attack her.

A chance to...

Grace turned around. Pointed the rifle back. But this time, at Rex. Not at Aoife.

"Don't even think about trying anything. I really, really don't want to have to kill a dog. Another dog, anyway."

She turned around again. Walked down the steps. And as much as Aoife wanted to resist her, as much as she wanted to fight her... she followed her.

Because she feared for Rex.

And she feared for what she was going to find, too.

She reached the bottom of the steps.

Saw Grace standing right at the back of the warehouse. Right by a door. An open door.

"Come on," she said.

Aoife wasn't sure she could get anywhere near her without ripping her fucking face off.

But the gun pointed at Rex.

And that threat of something happening to Hailey. To Geoff. All looming over her.

She reached the door.

Looked inside.

Heart racing.

Body totally tense.

When she saw who was in there, she froze.

Hailey was on her knees. Bind around her mouth. Tears streaming down her face. Blood trickling from her forehead.

But it was the person behind her who really caught Aoife's eye.

The man standing there.

Pistol in hand.

Pointed right at Hailey.

"Hey, Aoife," Geoff said. "I'm sorry about this. Really, I am. But she left me with no choice."

CHAPTER TWENTY-THREE

Aoife saw Geoff standing there, pistol to Hailey's head, and she couldn't quite believe what the hell she was seeing.

Hailey was on her knees. Gagged. Tears streaming down her cheeks. Her eyes looked dark, and her hair looked a mess. Looked like she'd been through shit on her way here.

But it was the sight of Geoff behind her that really got to Aoife. Because she'd grown to trust the guy. Hadn't started off that way. Didn't particularly like him at first. Okay, didn't particularly like *anyone* at first.

But Geoff in particular, she'd changed her opinion of. He was a bit set in his ways. But he seemed a reasonable bloke underneath all that macho exterior.

And seeing him like this now... she just couldn't make sense of it.

She even forgot about her animosity towards Grace, just for a moment.

"What the hell?" was all she could say.

Geoff had a pistol right against Hailey's temple. His eyes were wide, and he looked at her like he was having a hard fucking time here. Like he was sorry.

But it wasn't enough. Because he was working with the enemy. He was working with the woman who'd destroyed her home. Who'd killed Max.

And for that, she felt nothing but rage.

"I know it's hard to get your head around. But—"

"Hard to get my head around?" Aoife said. Barely able to contain her composure. "Hard to get my *head* around? That's all you can say? Really?"

"Aoife—"

"This woman destroyed our community. She killed Max. And she..."

It hit her, then. Hit her like a punch to the gut.

"Someone held me back," Aoife said. "Someone... someone stopped me from getting to Max. Stopped me from helping him. From saving him."

Geoff looked away. And it was that look away that told Aoife all she needed to know.

"It was you."

"It wasn't easy," Geoff said. "Max was... Max was a good man."

"How can you say that?" Aoife shouted. Inching forward. It was only that gun to Hailey's temple that stopped her moving any further. "How—how can you say that when you let him die? When you watched all our people die?"

"What I did wasn't easy, Aoife. But neither was what happened that day here at the warehouse. What you did. To all their people."

"Bullshit," Aoife shouted. "You stood there with me. You were as much in it as I was."

"And I've felt fucking terrible about it ever since," Geoff said. "It's haunted me. Kept me awake at night. And when I got wind about Grace, out in the woods... when I ran into her, I knew I had to make amends."

Aoife couldn't speak. She couldn't wrap her head around what she was hearing.

"She had me on my knees. She made me beg for a second chance. And I told her I'd help. I told her I'd do whatever the hell I could to help. Because what we did to 'um... sick as they are, they didn't deserve that."

Aoife thought back to standing there, looking down at that circle of flames. She thought of Geoff, there behind her. At the time, she wanted to believe he'd looked down with hatred. But now, when she thought back, she wasn't sure he looked down at all. Wasn't sure he could.

"So what?" Aoife said. "You're with her now? With her on her revenge mission? That's it?"

"I promised her I'd help her get what she wants. Then... then she'll help me get what I want."

"And what's in it for you?"

"Geoff's family went missing a long time ago," Grace said. "Karen. And his daughter, Coleen. I can help him find them again. Because I know where they are."

"And that's it?" Aoife said. "Destroying our entire community for that bullshit?"

"It's not bullshit," Geoff said. Shaking his head. Visibly crying now. She'd never seen him like this before, and she didn't like what she saw. "It's... If they're out there, if there's even a tiny chance they're out there, then it's worth it."

She heard Geoff's words and realised just how little she knew this man. How little she knew about the pain he'd been through. How much he'd covered it up. How many secrets he'd kept.

"So go on," Aoife said. Shaking. Barely able to stand. "How long have you two been in bed together?"

"Geoff helped me acquire the explosives I needed. And he helped me plant them, too. After that... well. It was just a case of timing it right. Absolutely right."

Aoife looked over at Geoff and shook her head. At Hailey, in front of him, tears rolling down her face from her bloodshot red eyes. "How could you do this? You were supposed to be one of us."

"I'm sorry," Geoff said, crying too. "But if there's any chance my family are out there—"

"She's using you. Don't you see that? Your family is gone. And you know what? They're better off without you."

"No!" Geoff shouted.

He yanked Hailey closer to him.

Buried the gun deep into her temple.

Tears spilling out now.

"They're still out there," he said. "They have to be. And she can help. Grace can help. And this... this is what we deserve. It's what we deserve. For what we did. For everything that happened."

Aoife looked into Geoff's eyes. And all the hate she'd felt towards Grace, she felt it towards Geoff now, too.

"You'll pay for this," Aoife said. "Both of you. You'll pay for this."

She looked around at Grace.

Standing there with her rifle pointed at her.

Face covered.

Those eyes, staring at her. Piercing.

She looked at Geoff.

At Hailey, shaking, crying.

"I'll make sure you never get away with this. I'll make sure you never—"

And then Aoife heard a bang.

CHAPTER TWENTY-FOUR

Aoife heard a bang, and immediately closed her eyes.

That bang. Right in front of her. She didn't want to see it. Didn't want to see Hailey slumped on the floor. She'd heard something thud. Something fall to the floor. And the thought that it was Hailey filled her with hatred, filled her with dread. Because Hailey didn't deserve this. Nobody deserved this.

But at the hands of Geoff, too.

The bastard. The traitorous bastard.

He deserved all the bad things that were coming his way.

All the bad things that Aoife was going to bring to him.

And then she heard something, right ahead.

First, Rex by her side. Growling.

Then whimpering.

A whimpering that sounded like... Hailey?

She opened her eyes and couldn't believe what she was looking at.

Hailey was still kneeling there. Gag around her mouth. Crying.

But she was covered in blood.

And behind her, she could see someone lying there.

Kicking out.

Writhing around on the floor.

Geoff.

He was bleeding out from a hole in his neck. Clutching that hole, trying to stop the blood flow. His eyes were wider and more bloodshot than Aoife had ever seen.

He reached out. Clawed at the air.

Grace stood over him. Rifle in hand. Pointed down at him.

"You served me well," she said. "But you're a dumb fool. A dumb fool who betrayed his people the second a shred of hope was thrown your way. You weak, weak man."

She pointed her rifle, right at his shaking head. Thick, dark blood still pouring out between his fingers.

"But you did a good thing for me. It can't bring back my people. It can't bring back my brother. But you helped me. And for that, I'll be forever grateful. But you stood by her side. And for that..."

She pulled the trigger.

The bang echoed through the warehouse.

Geoff's head exploded, right there on the floor.

Aoife stood there and watched. Watched the blood pool out of Geoff's neck. Watched Hailey sitting there on her knees, kneeling, eyes shut, crying. That fear clearly inside her; that fear she was next.

And Grace standing there. Rifle in hand.

Standing over Geoff.

She looked up at Aoife, and as much as Aoife wanted to launch herself at her, as much as she wanted to chase her...

She saw the way Grace lifted the rifle.

Pointed it at her.

And she knew there was only one thing she could do right now.

She turned, and she ran.

"Come on, Rex!"

They ran together. Away, through the door.

Heard a blast.

A blast crack against the wall beside her.

"Rex, quick!"

But Rex was standing his ground.

Kicking back.

Barking at Grace.

And she had her rifle pointed at him.

Aoife jumped back.

She dragged Rex out of the way.

And then she realised she was standing there, in the way of Grace's rifle.

She stood there. Blocking Rex. Shielding him. Hailey was nowhere to be seen.

Just Grace.

Just Grace and her rifle and her opportunity. Her chance.

She saw that look in her eye.

Hatred.

But also... hesitation.

She didn't hesitate herself.

She spun around and ran.

Another blast.

Another gunshot, narrowly missing her.

Saw the door ahead of her.

The door out to the wild.

The door out of this place.

A chance of escape.

She ran as fast as she could, the sound of footsteps approaching. Wanted to go back for Hailey. Wanted to help.

But she knew there was no chance.

She had to just keep going.

She had to get Rex out of here.

She reached the door. Dragged Rex outside. Turned around,

saw Grace standing at the other side of the warehouse. Rifle pointed right at her now.

She pulled the trigger.

A click.

A blank.

That realisation in her eyes.

That look towards her rifle.

A moment Aoife had to take.

She turned around and, Rex by her side, she did what went against all her instincts.

Because all her instincts were still to hunt this Grace down and make her pay, even if it was the last thing she did.

But she turned.

And she ran.

CHAPTER TWENTY-FIVE

Grace watched Aoife run into the distance through the scope of her rifle, dog by her side, and she tightened her finger on the trigger.

Seeing her here. Seeing her running away. She felt a whole mixture of emotions about everything that'd happened. Because she hated her. She wanted to put her through hell. She wanted to make her suffer. She wanted her dead.

But at the same time...

She'd had an opportunity to shoot her. Plenty of opportunities to shoot her.

And she'd either missed, or she'd frozen.

Coward. Absolute fucking coward. Because she'd killed so many people, all in the name of getting to Aoife. She'd done so many horrible, awful things, all in the name of revenge.

And yet when it actually came to Aoife—when it came to the woman who'd looked her in the eye while around her, the rest of her people burned—she couldn't act.

What did that say about her?

What did that make her?

She watched Aoife disappear further into the trees, dog by her side. And as much as in any ordinary situation, this might seem like the final time they'd meet... Grace knew that wasn't the case.

They'd meet again.

Aoife would come for her. Or she'd go for Aoife.

They were connected now. Connected, like magnets.

And they'd keep on drawing towards each other. Because they both wanted the same thing from each other.

And yet...

The more Grace thought about how close she'd been to killing Aoife, the more she thought about how much she hated her, despised her... the more she remembered the woman she used to be in the world before.

Caring for kids with special needs. How much she got from her job. How much purpose she got from it. How she put it before anything else.

And how caught up she'd got with Christopher and his people.

The *shame* she felt about how caught up she'd got with Christopher and his people.

How out of hand it'd all got. But how she'd just done what she'd done, quietly, hoping to break free eventually. Hoping for a better opportunity, eventually.

Getting that opportunity, then Aoife taking it away from her. Completely.

She watched Aoife disappear completely behind the trees. Lowered her rifle, turned around, walked back inside the warehouse.

She saw Hailey standing there right away.

She was holding something.

The pistol Geoff had dropped.

Grace sighed.

Lowered her rifle.

"Looks like I got a bit complacent, doesn't it?"

She walked towards Hailey, who stood there, hands shaking. Still crying.

Walked towards her with confidence.

Hailey backing away, even though she was holding a gun.

Shaking her head.

Like she was trying to stop Grace walking towards her.

Pleading with her.

"Go on," Grace said. "If it's what you want to do... pull the trigger. I'd understand it. After what I did to..."

It all happened so fast.

Hailey pulled the trigger.

The gun clicked.

No bullets came out.

Hailey's face dropped.

Grace sighed. "You really think I'd give a snake like Geoff a loaded gun? Really?"

Hailey backed away even more now. But there was nowhere she could go.

Grace kept walking towards her.

Lifting her balaclava from her head.

Watching the horror spread across Hailey's face as she saw her, standing there, backed into a corner.

She looked into her eyes.

Stood there, right over her.

"You're the same," Grace said. "The lot of you. Cowards."

And then she grabbed Hailey by the side of the head.

Grabbed her, and instead of seeing Hailey there, she saw Aoife there.

"You came in handy. But you've served your purpose."

* * *

It's a good job Hailey had a gag on.

Because otherwise, Aoife would have heard her screams from a mile away.

CHAPTER TWENTY-SIX

A oife didn't stop running until she was absolutely sure Grace wasn't following her anymore.

She crouched in the woods, behind a few trees, staring down at the warehouse. She couldn't slow her heart rate down for anything. Her breathing wasn't much better. Grace hadn't fired any bullets at her for a while. She'd stepped back inside, disappeared from sight.

And all Aoife wanted to do was go down there. Take Grace the fuck down. She still couldn't quite believe what'd happened. Getting there. Finding Grace. Hearing Grace's side of the story, her version of events.

Then Geoff.

Geoff with his gun to Hailey's head.

Grace shooting Geoff...

Then her and Rex running, escaping, fleeing...

She thought of the way Grace stood there, pointing that rifle at her. That momentary hesitation, where she'd been able to run away. The bullets crashing into the walls and the floor around her, but never quite hitting her.

For a moment, Aoife wondered why she hadn't been more

accurate with her shots. But then it struck her. It struck her in a way that made total sense.

She wanted to keep Aoife alive.

She wasn't done torturing her yet.

Aoife looked down at that warehouse. Rex lay by her side, on his front, panting. She was trying to take deep breaths. Trying to calm herself. But she couldn't see past what Grace told her.

About what Aoife did to her.

To her people.

And how not all of those people were as evil and savage as Aoife wanted to believe they were, as much as they'd done godawful things.

But no. Those bastards were cannibals. They gave up any right to any kind of forgiveness when they started eating people.

There's no way Aoife could've gone along with shit like that. She'd be out of there at the first opportunity.

But what if there hadn't been an opportunity?

What if she'd had no choice, and the only way to survive was to toe the line and wait for the perfect chance to get out? To start again?

She shook her head. She couldn't keep thinking that way.

She couldn't feel guilt, and she couldn't feel regret.

The only thing she could feel was rage.

Rage towards the bitch who'd done this to her.

Rage towards the bitch who'd murdered Max and murdered all her people.

She thought about Geoff. Fucking fool. He should've known better than to fall for that bullshit about his family.

But then she thought about what he'd said. About hope.

Would she have been any different in his shoes, really?

If she caught wind that someone *she* cared about was out there, wouldn't she go to any lengths to find them?

Even if there was no evidence at all?

No. Not that far. Never that far.

But then she thought about what she'd done to Grace's people.

People she didn't even dare to consider the circumstances of.

She'd just seen them all as the same cannibalistic scum as Christopher. But already, as much as it pained her to admit it, she knew that wasn't the case.

Because Christopher's people were the ones who'd lowered their weapons.

Who'd let the people of the estate go.

And now they were all dead.

Now *all* of them were dead.

And it was all on her.

She felt her heart skip a beat. Gasped for a breath. Her head spun, and her body shook. She gritted her teeth, and she curled up into a ball.

Because as much as she tried to hide the thoughts, as much as she tried to suppress them, as much as she tried to run from them... the reality was right there, staring her in the face, inescapable.

The estate was gone because of her.

Max was dead because of her.

She shook her head and cried into her knees. Beside her, she could hear Rex whining. She wanted to comfort him. She wanted to stroke him. She wanted so, so much.

But then she felt that old demon of not wanting to connect with anyone resurfacing again. Because Rex was in danger, too. Rex was in danger, and if Grace had her way, Aoife was going to lose everything—before losing herself.

But not before a world of torture.

But then Aoife felt a tightness in her gut.

A sudden bolt of realisation.

No.

This wasn't on her.

Aoife might've done the savage thing. But she'd done it because those people *were* savages.

And Grace's response to what'd happened—the way she'd slaughtered so many innocent people—only went to prove Aoife's point even more.

She stood up. Wiped her eyes. Took a deep breath of the cold winter air. Stared right down at that warehouse.

She was going to hunt Grace down.

And she was going to make her pay for what she'd done.

She wasn't the prey.

Not anymore.

She was the predator.

She gritted her teeth, tightened her fists.

Every instinct in her body made her want to walk down there towards that warehouse.

But she had to be cleverer than that. Smarter than that.

And one thing was for sure.

She knew Grace wasn't going to give up on her.

So she could use that to her advantage.

She took another deep breath, looked down at the warehouse, then turned away.

"Come on, Rex. There's somewhere we need to go."

CHAPTER TWENTY-SEVEN

Aoife waited until dark before she went back to the estate.

It felt strange being back here. Sad. The flames had gone out, but there was still the smell of smoke in the air, the taste of burning. Every now and then, she swore she heard sounds —footsteps, rustling, voices. Crows cawing. And the thought of them swooping down and eating the charred remains of so many people made her feel sick.

But she'd watched this place for a good while now.

And she knew exactly where she needed to go in order to load up and gather some supplies for the next stage of her journey.

She stood there, right by the gates of the west wall. The entire wall had been shattered with the explosions. She had to clamber over the brick and the debris to get over. Every now and then, she felt something nudge against her foot, realised it was a limb. A loose hand or an exploded leg. A reminder of all that'd happened here. Everyone she'd lost.

She felt that guilt surfacing again.

That guilt for her own hand in this.

That knowledge that vengeance and lust for revenge had got her into this mess...

Then she pushed it away.

Fuck that shit.

Grace deserved whatever she was going to get.

She hopped down off a pile of bricks and stood in the middle of the dark street.

Usually at night, the place was quiet. But this felt different. It felt ghostly. Dead.

There was nobody around at all.

The sound of a shop door creaking in the cold breeze.

Bodies lining the road.

Bricks and debris everywhere.

She walked through the street, keeping her head down, keeping her sadness at bay. Trying to stay in the moment. Trying not to get caught in the guilt. In the sadness. In the hatred.

Just walking to where she needed to go.

She went towards the end of the terraced street, past the houses that so many people called home, and saw the old mechanics up ahead.

She knew there were weapons there. Not many, just stuff they'd found on their supply runs, their scouting missions. Generally, they tried to keep rifles and shit like that out of the hands of the people.

But Aoife knew there was enough in there with plenty of ammo after what happened with Christopher's people. Enough to at least be able to put up some kind of fight in case any shit like that ever happened again.

She went to the door. Tried to open it, but it was locked.

Walked over to the window.

When she got to the window, she noticed something.

The window was smashed. And it didn't look like it was smashed by the explosion, either.

It looked like it'd been smashed by someone who'd come here.

She looked around at the darkened streets. She'd seen the scavengers approaching earlier, and she knew she had to be careful. Was pretty damned sure all was good on that front, though. It looked all clear. Had to be.

"Come on, Rex," she said. "The sooner we get out of here, the better."

She climbed in through the window. Dropped inside the dark, empty mechanics. Definitely empty in here. Everything was so quiet. So silent. So echoey.

She walked across the floor, into the darkness, towards the room at the back, where she knew the supplies were kept. Reached it, and went to open it, when her stomach sank.

The door was locked. Of course it was frigging locked.

She took a few breaths, calmed herself. Gus usually ran this place. She had no idea where he'd be if not here. Either he'd run, or he'd been blown to pieces.

She'd have to find those pieces. Have to find those keys attached to him, wherever they were.

She went to turn back and head to the window when she saw movement outside.

She froze.

Totally still.

Heart racing.

Rex growling.

"Ssh," Aoife said.

She'd seen someone rush by. Definitely seen someone.

Unless it was a bird.

Or her eyes playing tricks on her.

She kept low. Walked over towards the window again, slowly. Held her breath and looked outside.

The streets were empty.

Dark.

No one in sight.

She took another deep breath. *Just your mind playing tricks on you. Find Gus somehow. And if not... find another way in. And failing that... fuck. You'll figure something out.*

She went to climb out of the mechanics, out into the street, when she saw the movement again.

Up the road.

She froze.

Three figures.

Three figures in black, two of them holding knives, and one of them holding a rifle.

Her skin turned cold.

Scavengers.

CHAPTER TWENTY-EIGHT

oife saw the scavengers walking through the middle of the estate, and she knew she was in deep shit if she didn't get away from here.

Fast.

She backed up slowly. Looked over her shoulder. Debris blocking the route out of here completely.

Her only way out of here, blocked.

And those scavengers, with their knives and their rifle...

She looked at the broken window by her side. The one she'd climbed through, into the mechanics.

If she could get back in there, maybe she could lay low.

Maybe she could hide.

But she had to be careful. Because even though it was dark, those scavengers were close.

And Rex's growling wasn't exactly helping.

"Rex," Aoife whispered.

But he wasn't for stopping at all.

"Rex!" Aoife said, a little sterner this time. "Come on. With me. Now."

She walked slowly towards the window, keeping her eyes on the scavengers at all times. Not for a second turning from them. She wanted to know right away when they saw her. She wanted to know exactly when to run.

She reached the window. Eased Rex through. Went to climb in...

That's when she saw them.

They turned over towards her.

One of them spoke: "Someone's there!"

She didn't even look anymore.

Didn't even think.

She just threw herself inside the mechanics and backed over to the wall.

She stood there in the darkness. Listened to those footsteps racing closer and closer towards the mechanics. She was trapped. She was trapped in here, and she was fucked.

No.

She couldn't be defeatist.

She couldn't give up.

She was stuck here. And if she was stuck here, then she had to fucking do her best to do something about it. Make the best of a bad situation and all that.

She looked around for a weapon. For something she could use. She was in a mechanic's, after all, so she'd surely find something.

She scrambled around for a tool. Something heavy. Something she could whack any fucker who stepped in her way over the head with.

Looked around as those footsteps got closer and closer but to no avail.

Then she saw it.

A hammer, right at the other side of the room.

She went to bolt towards it when she heard the footsteps right outside the window, and she knew they were here.

She dropped to the floor. Right behind a rusty old car. Heard the panting at the window. Rex being particularly quiet now, bless him.

"You see anyone in there, Kent? Or are those dumb eyes playin' tricks on you again?"

"Piss off, Serge."

"What was that?"

"Nothin'. Doesn't matter. I'll have a look anyway."

She couldn't see him, but she could hear him.

Climbing through the window.

Landing inside.

And she knew right then she wasn't alone, and she had to be quiet.

Extra fucking quiet.

He walked across the floor. Broken glass cracking underfoot. She moved around the car with Rex by her side, trying to keep out of his view at all times. She could see the window. If she could just get to it, she could climb out. She could make a break for it. Run.

She could see that hammer at one end of the room. Too far away. The scavenger too close to it.

And then...

The glass.

The broken glass.

She looked down and saw it, just metres away.

Fuck. Why'd she been so stupid? She could've grabbed a shard of glass and used that from the off.

She stared at that glass shard across the floor. If she could just reach it...

She heard Rex growl around the other side of the car.

"The hell was that?" the bloke—Kent—muttered.

Fuck. Could you not be quiet for one damned second, Rex?

She heard Kent walk around the side of the car, and she saw she had an opportunity. A chance.

Grab the glass.

Bury it into his throat.

Deal with the rest in her own time.

She went to make a break for the glass when she heard Kent laugh.

"Hell, boys. One damned tasty calendar in here! Full of tits, too!"

Aoife held her breath. Held Rex close. Her heart pounding like mad. Kent was so close. He was so close, and the glass was so close.

"You finished wanking in there, Kent? Or are you gonna get your arse out here? There's fuck-all here we haven't already got. Shit weapons, shit food, shit everything. Let's just leave. William'll be wondering where we're at."

She heard Kent sigh, flipping the pages of the calendar, then walk across the room to the window.

"Yeah, yeah," he said. "I'll be there in a sec, killjoys."

She saw him walk past her, knife in hand.

Saw him reach that window.

Watched him drop outside, disappear into the night.

When she was absolutely sure he was out of sight, she stood up.

Walked over to the window.

Went to stick her head outside.

That's when she felt it.

The man, Kent, grabbing her.

Dragging her out of the window and into the road.

She struggled. Swung the broken glass towards his ankle. Caught him just a little.

He let out a cry. Then he kicked her fingers hard, smashing the glass.

He dragged her. Lifted her by the throat.

Pressed his knife against her neck.

Looked at her with his fat face, his breath reeking like shit, and he smiled.

"Well, well," Kent said, as Rex barked like mad beside them. "What *do* we have here?"

CHAPTER TWENTY-NINE

Aoife felt Kent's hands tightening around her throat and gasped for breath.

He had tight hold of her. Real tight hold of her. And he was strong, too. So strong that her feet hovered above the ground. She could see Kent standing there, that smirk on his big fat face of his. Behind him, she could see his two friends, one of them holding a rifle, pointing it at her. The other just standing there, scanning her from head to toe, eyeing her up. Creep.

Beside her, she could hear Rex barking. And she wanted him to stop. She knew what scavengers could be like sometimes. Hell, she knew what *people* could be like.

She didn't want him provoking them into doing anything horrible.

She didn't want to lose anybody else.

"You're not as smart as you think, y'know?" Kent said. "Heard you sniffing around the second we got here. Saw you creepin' about, too. A woman, on her own. That's dangerous, y'know?"

Aoife wanted to punch the bastard, to put him in his place. Creepy, misogynistic fuck.

"But it's okay, honey," Kent said. "I get it. Just seein' what's been left behind here. I get it. We all get it. That's why we're here, too. Only... well. Let's just say I didn't expect to find somethin' quite so tasty on the menu."

He laughed. And the blokes behind him laughed, too. And Aoife knew the only way through these creeps was by violence. She felt an idiot. A fucking idiot for coming back here when she knew the scavengers were around. But all that shit with Grace... needing to find weapons. Needing to trap her somehow...

All of it was just playing havoc with her mind.

She didn't have a proper plan. She just had this raw desire for revenge surging through her system.

This guilt.

This shame.

And this hatred.

And it'd got her caught in this shit.

"What's yer name, sugar? Speak to me."

Aoife tried to open her mouth, tried to speak, but she couldn't say a word. Kent's grip around her neck was too tight. Everything was growing hazy, blurry.

"Loosen your grip on her a little, Kent. She ain't no good to no one dead."

"Huh," Kent said. "I don't mind 'um dead. Less... scratchy."

His eyes glistened.

She noticed a hardness right around his crotch.

And she knew exactly what kind of a creep this bastard was.

But then he loosened his grip. Loosened it, and she fell to the road. Smacked her knees against the concrete. Coughed, gasped, and spluttered for air.

She looked up. Saw Rex beside her, nudging her like he wanted her to get to her feet. Like he wanted her to stand.

"See, one thing I will say," Kent said, walking around in front of her. "Your dog here. He's a good'un. Protective. I like that."

And then he pulled back his knife and launched himself at Rex.

"No!" Aoife shouted.

She threw herself in front of him.

Dragged him down to the ground, covering every inch of his body.

Kent stopped, comically, just feet away from her. Laughed, like he was just fucking with her all along. Lowered his knife. "Hell, I'm just messin' with ya. Wouldn't hurt a dog. Unless it hurt me, anyway. Different matter altogether, then."

"Stop dicking around, Kent," one of the other blokes said. Serge, Kent called him before. "We need to get out of here. We need to get back to camp. It's late as it is."

Kent sighed. "Killjoy. Always a goddamned spoilsport. Well, come on, love. Let's get you on yer feet. There ain't shit here for us. But you'll do as a prize. You'll more than do. The boys are gonna love you—"

"What if I told you there's weapons here?" Aoife said.

Kent frowned. The other two looked bemused. "Huh?"

Aoife gulped, her throat still sore from before. "What if... what if I told you I'm from this place. I was from here before it was burned down. And—and I came back because I was after a weapon. To fight someone. The people... the person who did this?"

Kent frowned. "In English, love?"

"That mechanics," Aoife said, pointing towards it. Not really knowing the full lengths of her plan but knowing damned well she needed to think on her feet. Fast. "The one I was in. I went there because behind the locks in there, there's a storeroom. And in that storeroom, there's weapons. Only it needs a key. A key I don't have. But you... you could help me find it."

Kent looked back at the other two, then at her again. "Still not quite followin'"

"A man called Gus used to run this place. He lives... he lived in that house just opposite. If we can find his keys, we might be able to get in there. We might be able to get those supplies."

She said these words and saw the way they were looking at her. Like she had a motive.

And she *did* have a motive.

She knew Gus didn't live in that house opposite.

But that house *was* in dire need of construction work.

And if she could somehow get them in there, she could use its collapsing form to her advantage.

She just needed to persuade them.

"I won't pretend we had loads of arms," Aoife said. "But we had enough. Enough that you'll be interested. Enough that you won't want to ignore it. I'm sure of it. So please. Let's... let's go to Gus' place. And if we find his keys... Well, you can do whatever you want to do with me after that. But at least give me a chance."

Kent looked back again.

Then looked around at Aoife.

Smirked.

"That's a sweet proposal, love. But can I tell you one thing?"

He walked right up to her.

Leaned in towards her ear.

"I don't take orders from no bitch."

The next thing Aoife knew, he had one arm around her throat and a hand around her mouth, and he was dragging her away.

CHAPTER THIRTY

Grace watched the three men surround Aoife and her barking dog, and a strange feeling of jealousy came over her.

She saw the way the big bloke held her up by the throat.

Saw the way the other two scanned her up and down, head to toe, like she was a piece of meat.

She saw it all, and she didn't feel sympathy for her. Didn't feel pity for her.

But she felt jealousy. Envy.

Because she wanted Aoife all to herself.

She saw the man loosen his grip on Aoife. Saw him drop her to the road. And then she watched her as she spoke. She could see her pointing. See her trying to beg.

And a part of her enjoyed this. A part of her enjoyed watching Aoife trying to wriggle out of this situation.

A part of her hoped they gave her the second chance she was so desperately pining for.

But then that other part of her went numb.

Especially when she saw the man walk up to Aoife.

When she saw him smile, then punch her across the face.

When she saw Aoife collapse in a heap.

And then the man lifted her up, carried her over his shoulder.

She watched, and she felt that rage burning inside. That desire —that need—for revenge.

Because Aoife was hers.

Aoife was all hers.

And she wasn't going to let her just slip away like this.

She watched the men take her away, and for a moment, she wondered if maybe letting these men do what they wanted with Aoife might be the best course of action after all.

Because at least that meant she'd go through hell.

She'd go through all kinds of pain.

But on the other hand... she felt a tightening inside her body.

A resistance.

Aoife was hers.

And she was going to make damned sure it was *her* who put her through the hell she deserved. Not some random fucking *men*.

CHAPTER THIRTY-ONE

Aoife felt dizzy.

She turned her head. Wherever she was, it was bright. So bright it hurt to open her eyes. Her first instinct was that she'd been drinking and had far too much last night.

But... no. This was different. This felt hazy.

This felt...

It hit her again, all at once.

Everything that had happened.

Max.

Grace.

Everything.

She opened her eyes again, instinctively, even though it pained her to do so.

It wasn't light at all. Wasn't bright. In fact, it was dark. Very dark. She could barely see a thing. Only she was in some kind of big room with a large window opposite. She could see the moonlight shining in from outside. That must've been what'd seemed so bright at first.

She closed her burning eyes. Her head ached like mad.

Fuck it. She needed to figure out what the hell was going on here.

Her wrists were tied. Typical. Her ankles didn't feel much freer, either. She was on some kind of chair. Uncomfy as hell. Why did people always have to throw you on an uncomfortable chair when they captured you? Like, wasn't the whole act of being captured enough in itself?

She scooted herself around in the chair, side to side, tried to get herself comfier. Knowing full well she had to figure out how the hell she was going to get out of this mess.

"No point fighting," a voice behind her said. "No point resisting. You're with us now. And you ain't gonna get out of it. So just accept that. It'll all go a whole lot easier for you if you do."

She didn't recognise this voice. It wasn't Kent or any of the twats from before that she could tell.

And she couldn't see whoever it was, either. He was right behind her. Keeping himself out of the way.

"You gonna stay behind me?" Aoife asked. "Or are you gonna look me in the eye?"

The man laughed. Slowly stepped out, right in front of her.

She couldn't see him properly in the moonlight, but she could make enough of him out to tell what kind of bloke he was. That long, greying hair, so greasy she could almost taste it in the air. The stench of his breath like something had died in there. And the sores all over his skin. Not the picture of health, let's put it that way.

"You've got some nerve," he said. "The boys told me about that."

"What the boys didn't tell you is how much I'm gonna enjoy killing you the first chance I get."

The man laughed again. Shook his head, scratching his grey locks. "You're somethin', I'll give you that. You've got fight, and you've got spirit. It's nice to see. But we'll work on that. We always do."

"Where's my dog?"

"Your dog? I don't remember seeing a dog."

Aoife felt instantly protective. "If you've done anything to him. Anything..."

"It's like I said. I don't remember seeing a dog."

"I don't know what your deal is, you creep," Aoife said, shaking. Almost at her fucking wits' end. "But when I get out of this chair—"

"You ain't getting out of that chair," the man said. Sounded sterner now. More assertive. "Well. You might. From time to time. But you're livin' by our rules now, sugar. And let me tell you somethin'."

He leaned over. Right to her ear. So close she was drowned in the stench of his acrid breath.

"Us guys, we have long, long days of work. We get tired. We get stressed. And when we get back... well. Let's just say we need to get the stress out of our system. And a beautiful lady like you... you'll help with that."

She spat at him. Right in his face.

He stepped back. Wiped the saliva from his face. Smirking, almost like he'd enjoyed it. "That's how you lot always react in the beginning. But in time... in no time at all... it's like I said. We'll work on that."

He turned around. Walked over to the side of the room, towards a door.

Looked back at her. That smirk still etched across his face.

"I'm William, by the way. I run this place here. And you and me are gonna get to know each other awful well over these next few days. And weeks. And months."

His smile widened, and she caught a flash of those yellow teeth, barely reflecting in the moonlight.

Then, he turned around, and he disappeared through the door, leaving Aoife in the darkness.

CHAPTER THIRTY-TWO

G race followed the footprints from the estate, in the direction the men had taken Aoife, and she swore she was being watched.

It was a very suburban area she was in, so it wouldn't exactly be majorly surprising if there was someone else around. She could see the big, detached Victorian houses alongside the road on one side. On the other, the old hospital. A maternity ward, once upon a time. Big long building with huge windows. It always looked derelict and unlived in. Spooky as hell.

But now, in this world without power, it looked more empty and more derelict than ever.

She knew the men were around here somewhere. She held her rifle close. She'd found some ammo back at the warehouse. Loaded up. Not many bullets.

But hopefully, she wouldn't need many anyway.

She just needed to get in there.

Get Aoife out, somehow.

Because Aoife was hers. And she wasn't going to let anybody else near her.

She walked further down the road when she saw movement behind one of the windows at the old hospital.

There was someone in there. It was only slight, only momentary, but definitely a figure in there.

Shit. She needed to lay low. Needed to keep a low profile. Last thing she wanted was to draw attention to herself, out here on her own.

She went to walk further down the street when she heard movement behind her again.

She turned.

Didn't see anyone.

But she knew she was being watched. Just that sense that someone was here with her. Someone was close.

She had to be careful.

She had to watch her step.

She went to turn around again when she saw a figure in the shadows.

She froze.

Lifted her rifle.

Really didn't want to have to use it. Especially not yet. One pull of that trigger and the sound would be enough to radiate around the whole damned street.

But if someone was here, if someone was stalking her, if someone was close...

She had to be willing to do anything.

She walked back. She had to find whoever it was. She had to deal with them. She couldn't have them stalking her.

She reached the road she'd seen the figure disappear down.

Stood by the old post office on the edge of the street. Hands shaking. Heart racing.

Fuck it. Here goes nothing...

Then she stepped around the corner and pointed her rifle.

She saw the figure right away.

Saw the source of the movement.

And when she saw it, she froze.

It wasn't a man. It wasn't a person at all.

It was a dog.

She went to turn away from it, went to leave it, when she noticed something.

Something struck her about this dog.

It was familiar.

And then it hit her.

Aoife's dog.

The Rottweiler she'd seen following her everywhere.

It was him. It had to be him. Couldn't be a coincidence.

She was half-tempted to put a bullet through its skull. To shoot it, right here and right now.

And another part of her wanted to keep him with her so she could get to Aoife—and then, when the time was right, punish her even more.

But there was something stopping her.

The memory of her own dog.

Wilson.

Golden Retriever.

How loyal he was. The good times they'd had together. The laughter. The warmth. The happiness.

And how broken she'd been when she'd lost him that day at the vet's, forced to have him put to sleep.

She felt herself welling up. Choking up. Remembered the sound of the barking and the howling inside the estate when she'd attacked. How guilty she'd felt. Guiltier than any person she'd caused pain.

She looked at this dog, and a part of her wanted to kill it. If just to get to Aoife.

But the part of her that remembered Wilson overrode everything else.

She lowered her rifle.

"Go away," she said. "Get the hell out of here."

She turned around, kept on walking.

Heard those nails on the tarmac behind her.

She stopped. Sighed. "Come on. I'm giving you a chance here. Don't push your luck."

But remarkably, he didn't stop following her.

She turned around. "Look, mutt. I killed your dad. And I'm really, really keen on killing your mum. Consider yourself lucky I'm even giving you a chance."

He tilted his head.

And despite her annoyance, despite her irritation, she actually laughed.

Shook her head and laughed.

"Dumb mutt," she said. "What are we going to do with you?"

She looked at him, and she pictured the kind of life he'd lived before. He looked pretty well looked after. He probably *was* well looked after.

And it brought back her guilt.

Her guilt over what she'd done to his home.

To his people.

She took a breath and sighed.

Remembered what those people did to her people.

Or more specifically, what Aoife did to her people.

She gritted her teeth.

Tensed her fists.

Turned around.

It all happened so fast.

First, the dog barking.

Then, the sound of someone shuffling before her.

Then, a hand around her mouth, and darkness.

CHAPTER THIRTY-THREE

Aoife had no idea how long she'd been locked away in this room, staring out of that large window ahead of her.

But she must've, by some miracle, dozed off at some stage. Because one moment, it was pitch black; the next, it was light.

She squinted out at the morning sun, beaming in through the window. There was condensation dripping down the glass. Outside, it looked frosty. Somewhere residential by the looks of things. Big field between her and the houses opposite. They looked big. Detached. Familiar, somehow. Maybe she'd gone down this road once upon a time. She wasn't sure. Probably. Looked like she was back in Preston, after all.

She was freezing cold. So cold her lips felt numb. Her face felt icy. Her ears and fingertips felt like they were going to drop off. She couldn't stop sniffing, couldn't stop shivering. She knew she needed to get the hell out of here and make the bastards who'd tied her up here pay for what they'd done.

But at the same time... that niggling sense.

She wasn't getting out of here.

She tried to pull against the binds around her wrists but with no luck. The ones around her ankles were just as tight, if not tighter. She gritted her teeth together. Her entire body tense. She wanted to shout out. Wanted to scream as the air before her frosted with her breathing.

She wanted to shout so loud that everyone in this place heard her.

But she knew she couldn't. Because that'd just draw everyone here.

And she needed to get out.

She pulled at the ties around her wrists again. Totally stuck. No way were they snapping. Fuck. She had to try another approach, another plan.

She took a few breaths, looked all around the room. There had to be something in here. Something she could use. The room was dusty. Empty. Looked like it'd been some kind of hospital, but a long time ago. Abandoned desks. Paperwork on the floor. Graffiti on the walls and foliage growing up the sides of the windows.

This place looked like it'd fallen into ruin a long time before the blackout hit. And it looked like the kind of place people might sneak into, kids with booze and drugs, urban explorers, those types. And if those types sneaked in here, and the place was in the kind of disarray it was in, then surely there had to be something nearby she could use? Something she could use to help herself escape?

Look, Aoife. Just fucking look. There has to be something. Use your brain. Don't admit defeat before you've even tried. When have you ever been a quitter?

She looked around the floor. Brick dust everywhere. No broken glass or anything, which she found remarkable considering the condition of this place.

She looked over at the old desks. At the dust-laden wooden surfaces. Tried to find something she could use. Anything.

But there was nothing.

"Fuck," she muttered. There had to be something around here. Something she could use. Anything...

That's when she saw it.

Behind her, on her left, she saw an old, loose piece of metal pipe. The edge looked pretty sharp. Sharp enough? She wasn't sure. But it was the sharpest thing in sight.

She tried to edge her chair back. Tried to force it back with all her weight, fully aware that one of the scavenger creeps could be in here with her, watching her, just taunting her.

But it didn't matter anyway. 'Cause the chair didn't budge.

"Come on..."

She tried again. Tried to edge back. And this time, she moved a little. Just a little.

Nowhere near close enough to the pipe. Nowhere near at all.

But progress.

That was the main thing.

She shuffled even further back. Towards that pipe. No idea whether this was going to work, but fuck it, what other choice did she have?

She had to keep going.

She had to keep trying.

She edged further and further to the back of the room when suddenly, she felt her chair shift just a little far back...

For a second, she hovered. Waited for the chair to go crashing to the floor.

Everything standing still.

And then she rebalanced, and the chair fell into place again.

Shit. That was a close call.

She took a deep breath. Edged further back. Heart racing. Sweat trickling down her, even though it was freezing cold in here. She knew she just had to keep trying. Keep focused.

She could do this. She'd been in worse situations than this

before, and she'd made it out. She wasn't going to let a bunch of scavenger pricks get the better of her.

She edged so close to the pipe that she was within touching distance. And it was just the right height for her to back against. To rub her wrists against. To try and break the ties.

She went to stretch out her wrists when she heard a bang somewhere to her right.

Then, footsteps.

She froze.

Turned around.

Fuck.

There was someone here.

Someone was coming.

She tried to shuffle forward, desperately tried to get back into place when suddenly she saw the man who ran this place—William—enter the room.

He looked over at her with a smirk on his face. Like he was unfazed by her runaway attempt. "Goin' somewhere?"

He laughed. Shook his head.

And he said something else, too.

Something Aoife couldn't make out.

Because all she could focus on was the woman here with him.

The woman he was dragging into the room.

"You're in luck," he said. "You've got yourself some company."

Aoife sat there, totally still, and stared into the eyes of a woman she didn't recognise.

Her face was burned. Badly burned. Her skin all veiny, all covered in angry red sores. Some of those sores were bleeding.

Her skin looked swollen, and her lips were purple.

She had barely any hair. Just a little strand dangling down the middle.

"Not as pretty as you," William said. "But hell. Put that bag over her head, and she's got a banging body."

Aoife couldn't think.

She couldn't speak.

She couldn't say a word.

Because the woman here in the room with her—the newly captured woman—was Grace.

CHAPTER THIRTY-FOUR

"Are we gonna just sit in silence like this?"

Aoife heard Grace's voice, and her entire body felt like it'd been electrocuted. She felt anger. She felt hatred. She felt pain.

But the hardest thing? The hardest thing of all?

The fact that she was so close to her, but she couldn't do anything to her. Because of the ties around her wrists and her ankles.

"Your dog's okay, by the way," Grace said.

"Shut up."

"Hey. I just wanted you to know. Well. It *was* okay, anyway. Stupid mutt followed me through the streets. I thought about shooting him. Really, I did. But you know what? I'm not a monster like you."

"You've got nerve after everything you've done."

"Trust me. The last place I want to be is here right now. And the last thing I want to be doing with you is *talking*. I want to make you suffer. I want to put you through a world of pain for everything you did to me. To our people. Because you see it now, don't you? Look at me. Look at me and look at what you did."

Aoife didn't want to turn. She didn't want to look at her. She didn't want to *see*.

But she couldn't help herself.

Grace was tied to a chair similar to hers, right opposite. Her face didn't match her voice. Not at all. There were the remnants of a woman there, somewhere. But her skin was all bumpy, the features all smoothed over. There were sores, too. Angry red sores and blisters. Her lips had been charred away. A few tufts of matted hair dangled from her bald head, here and there.

The only remnants of her humanity?

Those beautiful green eyes.

"I'm in pain all the time," Grace said. "And I don't just mean emotionally. I mean *actual* pain. I don't sleep at night because I can't close my eyes properly. I can't lie down because it feels like someone is cutting and cutting at my body, bit by bit. Like someone's burying a million hot needles into my back, my chest, right into the skin, right into the muscle, right into the bone."

"And I'm supposed to feel sorry for you? After the world of pain you've put so many through?"

"I'm not asking you to feel sorry for me. I'm just asking you to understand why I do this. Because the physical pain... the pain you can see for yourself... that's nothing compared to what I'm going through."

"So you keep saying," Aoife said.

"You have no guilt, do you? No remorse whatsoever? For what you did?"

Aoife sighed. She didn't want to give this woman anything. Didn't want to throw her a bone. "You were a member of a fucking vicious cult. What you did to people was unforgivable. And what you've gone on to do has only proven I should have finished the job."

"I don't think you really believe that."

"What?"

"Deep down, in your bones... I think it keeps you awake at night, what you did. At first, I thought you were this monster. I thought you were this savage. But you're not. And in a way... that makes it better, for me. Because I can see how I can hurt you. I can see exactly what I can put you through. Before I kill you."

Aoife looked into Grace's green eyes, and she thought about what she'd done.

The pain.

The screams.

And she thought about how right Grace was, about the guilt. As much as it pained her to admit it.

"I've felt guilty in the past," Aoife said. "I've... I've done things before that I'm not proud of. And I'll own them. But your people started this war. Your people started this. If you didn't want to risk what's happened, then you should never have done it in the first place."

Grace shook her head. "You just don't get it, do you? Or you just don't *want* to get it. Christopher wasn't the be all and end all of the group I came from. He was the leader. And there were people on board with him. But some of the people there were just following orders. Some of them were weak. Some of them were scared. And he preyed on that."

Aoife shook her head. 'Cause Grace was right. She didn't want to hear that.

Because it was a morally reprehensible move in the first place.

Knowing what she knew now—what Grace told her—it made those screams even harder to unhear...

"I see you're suffering," Grace said. "And that's enough for me. Right now, that'll do. But unfortunately, we've both found ourselves in the shit here. And the way I see it, that leaves us with only one choice."

"What are you talking about?"

"We need to get out of this place. And if we're going to get out of this place... we need to work together. We get out of here. We escape. And then when we're out of here... I'll kill you myself."

CHAPTER THIRTY-FIVE

William Bennett never liked women.

Especially since the first woman who was supposed to care for him—his "mother"—abused him and abandoned him when he was just a little lad.

Yeah. Hard to garner any kind of respect after something like that.

He'd persevered, though, you know? He'd grown up. He'd had girlfriends. But the same thing always happened, time and time again. No matter how nice he was, no matter how good he treated 'em, they always ended up betraying him. Stabbing him in the back. Time and time again.

Yeah, that sort of shit chipped away at your faith and your trust in the fairer sex.

But as far as he was concerned, they were good for one thing, and one thing only. He didn't have to go into detail with what he meant.

But the women they'd captured every now and then... they'd allowed the boys to release a bit of frustration.

And they'd allowed *him* to release a real load of frustration.

In an unconventional way, sure. But in a way that had always worked for him.

It started with one prostitute seven years ago. A crazy sex game gone wrong.

But he felt a buzz when it was done. Sick as fuck, sure. But a weird kind of buzz covering up the evidence. And getting away with it, too.

An unknown girl. Someone nobody searched for.

The following six times, it got easier and easier.

He remembered where he was when the power went out. A New Year's treat. Only he'd slipped up. Got caught stuffing her body into the boot of his car.

He remembered that fear. That fear of seeing that couple staring at him, and him staring back at them, and knowing that his game was up. Knowing that he had to do something drastic if he wanted to escape this.

And then he remembered the crashing sounds, the lights going out, and the whole world changing, all over again.

He smiled at the thought. God on his side. Clearly someone up there wanted him to continue his quest.

And that's exactly what he'd done.

Established a good little group of tough survivors. Blokes with similar interests. Okay. The rest of them not quite as savage as him, but they'd come round to his way of thinking. They were already halfway there, anyway. They knew what he got up to. They had to know it was weird how suddenly the women went missing.

They knew exactly what was going on.

But standing here, looking in through the crack in the door to the room where the women were, he felt a smile creep up his face.

Two of them.

Two of them landing right on his doorstep in one night.

One of them beautiful.

One of them... well. Not beautiful at all.

But it was that lack of beauty that drew him to her even more. That ugliness that awoke something inside him.

An animal urge.

An urge to dehumanise her, even more than whatever crazy-ass fire wounds she'd suffered had already damaged her.

He took a deep breath, swallowed a lump in his throat, and listened as they spoke together. As they tried to figure something out. Tried to escape.

He smiled at the hope in their muffled voices.

There was no way out of this for them.

And it was only going to get worse for them.

CHAPTER THIRTY-SIX

A oife sat in that seat, binds around her wrists, ties around her ankles, and she tried to get her head around Grace's suggestion.

"So let me get this straight," Aoife said. "You expect me to work with you, to get out of here? And then when we get out of here..."

"I kill you. Yeah."

Aoife shook her head. She had to give it to Grace: she was bold, and she was clear in her intentions. She wasn't fooling her into working with her to survive, only to stab her in the back. She was actively suggesting getting out of here and then finishing whatever business hung in the air between them.

"Or you kill me," Grace said. "I mean, I doubt that's how it'll go, I really do. You won't get that opportunity. But let's face it. I'd rather us settle our differences than die here, at the hands of these fuckers. Wouldn't you?"

Aoife looked around at her. And just seeing her made her stomach turn again. Not out of pure hatred. Because of course, there *was* hatred. But there was something else there. Seeing her burned skin. Seeing those bright green eyes beaming back at her. A glimpse of the beauty that was probably once there.

It made her feel a glimmer of pity.

And it made her feel guilty.

"You're right," Aoife said. "Much as it pains me to admit it... you're right. The last thing either of us want is for these fuckers to have their way with us. Not when... not when we've still got things to settle."

She thought she saw something like a smile stretch across her lipless face, just for a second.

"Good," Grace said. "I want to reassure you about something. I won't stab you in the back. I'll work with you. Because there's far, far more I want to put you through than these men can."

"The feeling's mutual," Aoife said.

"Then we do this professionally," Grace said. "We do this practically. We get out. And then we finish what we started."

Aoife didn't want to agree. She felt mad even contemplating agreeing with her. After all, this woman wanted to kill her. She wanted to exact more pain on her than these blokes here could do.

But at the same time... the only way they were getting out of here looked like by helping each other.

If there was even a way out at all.

They could get out of here.

And then they could settle their shit.

It wasn't going to be easy. It was going to take a lot of willpower.

But it might just be their best shot.

"Then what's your plan?" Aoife asked.

Grace's smile widened just a little.

Then she unfurled her lipless mouth, and something dropped out onto her thigh, covered in blood.

It was hard to make out at first. But the closer Aoife looked at it, the more she realised what it was.

It was a blade.

"How..."

"One of the perks of being burned to within an inch of your life? You don't feel stuff in certain places. Trust me, you feel a hell of a lot in other places. But here, the nerve endings, they're all burned away. My mouth's one area where that's the case. It's one of the few blessings of what you did to me. Makes me... stronger."

Aoife looked down at the blade on Grace's thighs, and she didn't know what she was suggesting, what she was implying.

"I can't reach it," Grace said. "You're going to have to scoot yourself over here. Lean back, grab it with your hands if you can. Then cut me free. Try anything—try to attack me first—and you'll regret it. You don't know how many more of these I have in here."

It dawned on Aoife then that Grace wasn't lying. The way blood trickled down her chin. The way she spoke, even more slurred than usual.

It wouldn't stun her at all if there were a ton of blades in there.

"And you really trust me not to try something?" Aoife asked. "Really?"

Grace smiled wider. "I think you hate me just as much as I hate you. I think you want to settle this far, far more violently than this. For what I did to that man of yours."

Aoife felt a visceral punch to the gut.

A reminder of the flames.

Of the cries.

A reminder of how much she hated this woman and how much she wanted revenge—proper revenge.

She dragged herself over. Pulled the chair along with her bodyweight, just like she had before. A few times, the chair toppled, felt like it was going to wobble over.

But she kept on going. Kept on forcing herself along.

Closer to Grace.

She reached the front of her chair and stopped, just for a moment.

Stared into Grace's eyes. Right into her face.

"I could kill you," Aoife said. "I could cut myself loose, and I could kill you."

Grace poked a blade out of her mouth. So long and so sharp that Aoife had no idea how she'd fit it in there and kept it in there.

Then she pushed it back in. The sharp edge of it catching quite visibly on the side of her mouth, to no reaction.

"You want to risk it? You have no idea how many more of these I have. Or where else I have them. Don't do anything silly, Aoife."

Aoife felt her skin crawl. "Bitch."

Then she leaned back, leaned towards Grace's chair, leaned towards the blade.

Leaned a little too far, and fell right back, supported only by Grace.

She felt something, then. Something sharp against her neck. From Grace's mouth.

"And now the tables are turned," Grace said. "Now, it's me in the position of power."

She laughed a little, then moved the blade away.

Aoife scrambled for the other blade, the one on her legs.

Tried to grab it. Tried to pick it up.

And eventually, she got it.

Eventually, she felt it.

She went to pull it away when she felt Grace's hands grab her.

"My wrists first."

Aoife held on to that blade. So close to pulling it away. So close to ramming it into her thigh.

And then she moved it back.

Moved it along her ties.

Sliced and sliced and sliced until...

She felt it.

Grace's hands fell free.

Tumbled forward as Grace pushed her away, then started working on her ankles with another of her blades.

"I'll see to you soon," Grace said.

But Aoife wasn't waiting around.

She cut at the ties around her wrists with the blade.

Cut more and more frantically as Grace tried to break free of hers.

She kept on cutting, constantly aware that Grace could just bury a blade into her at any moment... and then her wrists fell free.

She reached for the ties around her ankles.

Cut through them, even more frantically.

And then, when she broke free of them, she turned to Grace.

Saw her going to stand.

Saw the blade in her hand.

Went to stand too...

That's when Aoife heard it.

The door to the room, opening up.

Someone was here.

CHAPTER THIRTY-SEVEN

Aoife saw the door open, and every muscle in her body went numb.

There was a man at the door. Walking in the room. Not William, the apparent leader of this place. Someone else. Someone familiar.

The big guy. Kent.

He stood there, right by the door, and he had this animalistic look in his eyes. Almost like he didn't see her as human. Saw her as something less. Much less.

He had a belt in his hands, too.

A belt with metal spikes along it.

Tied around his palm and the back of his hand.

"Well, well," he said. "What do we have here?"

Aoife sat there, really still. She'd thrown herself back into her chair. Stuffed her hands around her back. Kept her legs right against the chair legs, so it still looked like there were ties around them.

And as far as she could tell, Grace had done the same.

What she hadn't been able to do, was scoot her way back to where she'd been sitting before.

She was still right there, in front of Grace's chair.

"What're you two up to? The boss never left you like this, I'm sure of it."

Aoife didn't say a word.

Just stayed sitting there.

Hands behind her back.

The blade tight in her grip.

Heart racing.

Palms sweaty.

Shaking all over.

"Hell," he said. "You've gone quiet. The pair of you have. You were a helluva lot more chatty when we ran into you."

"I've got nothing to say to you," Aoife said.

"Yeah," Grace added. "What she said."

Hearing Grace agree with her made her stomach turn. But still, it was something.

Kent walked over, across the large-windowed room, slowly. He had this smirk on his face. This smirk that seemed to grow even more the closer he got to the pair of them.

Tensing that belt around his hand, again and again, and again.

He reached Aoife. Stopped right in front of her.

She had to keep the blade tight in her grip.

She had to keep her legs close to the chair legs.

She had to make it look like she was still trapped.

She watched him stop right over her. Smelled his putrid onion breath. He was close. But he wasn't close enough for her to jump up. To attack him. He'd have too much of a window of opportunity to stop her.

"Nah, you're too quiet," he said. "Way too quiet for my liking."

He struck her on her thighs with the belt. Hard.

And every instinct in her body told her to shout. To let out a cry.

But she didn't want to show her pain to this bastard.

Kent laughed a little. "Good effort. Really is. Maybe we can make a habit of this."

He cracked the belt against her thighs again.

The pain was hot and sudden. Burning, stinging, aching really deep.

But still, she kept her cool.

Still, she kept her composure.

As calm as she could keep, even as tears stung her eyes.

He leaned into her then. Grabbed her hair.

And her instinct was to lift her hand.

To lift it and swing it at his throat.

He leaned into her face. Breathing that horrible breath all over her.

Smiling with those rotting teeth.

"The boss is looking forward to you," he said. "He's lookin' forward to the pair of you. But he told me to have a little fun with you myself first."

That creepy smile stretched wider.

His grip on her hair, harder.

He went to lift his belt, and she swung the blade towards his neck.

He stopped her.

Swatted away her hand, right in an instant.

The blade went tumbling across the room.

He looked over at the blade.

Then down at her.

Frown on his face.

Confusion, as the realisation kicked in.

"What..."

And then it clearly hit him.

He pulled back his fist.

Went to swing it at Aoife before she could bolt out of her chair.

Knocked her down to the floor.

She turned over. Head spinning. Ears ringing. Taste of blood in her mouth.

Looked around and up at him as she lay there on that hard, dusty floor.

He stood there with that belt in his shaking hand. Anger in his wide, bloodshot eyes.

"That was a bad move," he said, tightening the belt around his hand. "A really, really bad move."

He pulled back the belt.

Aoife braced herself.

And then she heard something.

A gasp.

The sound of flesh being pierced.

Of blood being gargled.

And a voice.

"She's mine."

She looked up.

Saw Grace standing behind Kent.

One of her blades buried deep into his neck.

She watched him slump to the floor, scrambling for his throat, desperately trying to stop the flow of blood.

Arm growing limper.

She watched him topple over.

Lie there on the floor, bleeding out, twitching.

And she saw Grace looking down at her.

Wiping her blade and sticking it into her pocket.

"Well," Grace said. "How about we get out of here?"

CHAPTER THIRTY-EIGHT

William walked down the corridor towards the room where they were keeping the women and wondered where the hell Kent was at.

He'd given him ten minutes. Ten damned minutes to do his worst. And sure, he knew what Kent was like. He knew he could push his luck sometimes.

But this... it'd been half an hour, maybe longer.

And the weirdest thing?

William hadn't heard any screams.

Which was especially weird where Kent was involved. Like he said, he knew what he was like.

"Where the hell're you at?" he muttered as he charged down the corridor, fists tensed. He was looking forward to dragging him out of there. Roughing him up a bit for breaching his rules. Sure, Kent was bigger than him. Kent was bigger than everyone.

But he knew where he stood in the pecking order.

Which made giving him a beating even more satisfying.

Even more liberating.

He reached the door when he noticed something and stopped.

There was blood on the floor, right by the door.

William paused a second. He had no idea whether that blood had been there already. Kind of lost track in a shithole like this.

It could just be blood from Kent doing his *thing*.

Or...

No.

It was impossible.

It couldn't be them.

He knocked on the door. Heard an echo amidst the silence. "Kent?"

Nothing.

He pushed the door open, not wasting any more time. Not holding back for anyone. Not giving a shit about what he might walk into, what he might find.

When he opened the door, he froze.

Kent lay there on the floor. His eyes were open wide. He was lying in a pool of his own blood.

The women were nowhere to be seen.

"Fuck," William said. He was going to have to alert the rest of the guys. Going to have to give them a heads up. Those women, they couldn't escape. How the hell had they been allowed to escape?

He marched out of the room, back towards the doors. "How the fuck did you let 'um get away, Kent? How the fuck could you be so fucking stupid?"

He walked out the room. Pushed open the door on the right, where he knew Dave and Wolfy would be.

"They've got out," William barked. "Kent let 'em get away, and you're tellin' me you didn't hear a thing? You're tellin' me..."

He stopped. Froze, again, completely.

Because he could see Dave and Wolfy.

But there was something wrong.

Both of them sat there in those chairs they always sat in, slumped over.

Both of their eyes had been gouged out. Dark red blood, all gungy, stuck to their cheeks.

William felt a shiver up his spine. Because he knew what'd happened here. And he knew who'd done this.

And if those two bitches had taken out Kent, *then* taken out these two idiots, then they'd have a free pass at escaping this place.

Just a case of running down the hallway.

Of going downstairs.

Of finding a window low enough to get out of.

He needed to stop them. This couldn't have happened long ago.

He needed to stop them—fast.

He turned around when he saw them standing there.

They were right there, right in front of him. Both of them. Together.

Blood on their hands.

Both of them looked at him with this expression on their face. Not a look of defeat. Not even a look of anger.

But a look of... accomplishment.

Of strength.

Almost like they were enjoying this.

And it gave William the creeps.

"Well," William said. "Quite the turn of events, huh?"

The pretty one, Aoife, came at him fast.

Lifting a blade.

"Ah," he said. "I wouldn't. Not if I were you. One shout and the rest of my men are here in a flash."

"Bold to assume the rest of your men are still alive," the feisty one, Grace, said.

William smirked at that. But for a second, he wondered. They couldn't have, could they? All his people? All his men? There were only eight of 'em. Smaller the group, the better. But now nine was six.

What if?

"So what happens now?" William said. "Sounds like you two have really thought this one through."

They looked at each other, the pair of them. There was this weirdness to how they looked at each other. Not in a friendly way at all. But like there was something there. A bond of some kind— a bond that William wasn't entirely sure was built on respect.

Then, they looked back at him.

"You know what happens now," Aoife said.

She stepped forward, and she rammed the blade into his throat.

He tried to push back. Tried to fight as the taste of iron filled his mouth. Tried to scramble free. Tried to bleed.

But then the other woman buried a blade in his chest.

And then the other one in his stomach.

And again and again and again, repeatedly as the strength drifted from him, as it melted away...

He hit the floor. Entire body in agony. Desperate to breathe. Desperate to fight.

But all he could do was lie there in that growing puddle of his own blood.

Vision fading.

Everything around him slipping away into the darkness.

And all he could do was stare up at those two women who'd done this to him.

Aoife spat on him.

Then, the other woman spat on him too.

"You made a mistake underestimating us," Aoife said.

Then she kicked him in the stomach, kicked him where he'd been stabbed, hard.

He let out a gargled yelp.

Then he saw the other woman, Grace, pull her foot back.

He saw it heading towards his face in slow motion.

He felt time slow down.

Felt his whole life flashing before his eyes.

And at that moment, at that single damned moment, William felt something more prominently than he'd ever felt in his entire life.

He felt sorry.

Grace's boot kicked him.

Pain.

Then, total darkness.

CHAPTER THIRTY-NINE

"So what now?" Grace asked.

Aoife looked down at William as he lay there on the floor. Beside him two more of his people. In the room they'd escaped Kent.

"We have no idea how many more he has," Aoife said.

Grace nodded, shrugged. "I'm sure we'll handle whatever he throws at us."

"But we need to be careful. We can't be complacent. We've got through the hardest part, but we can't let our guard down now."

Grace nodded again. Like she was taking on board what Aoife was saying. It was weird, really. Hearing her express this degree of approval. Working together with her. It just felt wrong. So, so wrong, after everything she'd done. After everything that'd happened. After all the baggage between them.

But they *were* in this together, this escape.

And in a weird way... Aoife knew Grace was right.

They had to get out of this place, because the pair of them deserved better than to die at the hands of these twats.

They had their own differences to settle. Their own baggage to resolve.

And whoever fell, whoever died, whoever was the victim... well, it didn't really matter just as long as one of them got their revenge.

That's what this felt like now.

"Either way, we need to get out of here," Aoife said. "Doesn't matter how we do it. Someone's going to find the bodies. And when they do, when they find out two of their prisoners have done this, they're going to be especially pissed."

Grace grunted a little bit at that. Almost sounded like a laugh.

"Wow," Aoife said.

"What?"

"Nothing."

"You said 'wow'. I'd appreciate it if you told me what that was about."

"It's just... well. I guess I've never heard you laugh before. Never heard you express any kind of happiness before."

Grace stared at her with those piercing green eyes. She didn't look amused. Or maybe that was just her face.

"I'm sorry," Grace said. "Making jokes with the woman who disfigured me beyond recognition and slaughtered my people doesn't exactly come easily."

Aoife looked down. "Yeah. My bad. Don't know why I said it. Can we go back to hating each other now?"

"I was joking," Grace said.

"Oh. It's... it's kind of hard to tell sometimes. Anyway..."

She walked past Grace. She didn't like this exchange. It felt too cordial. Too polite. Too... human.

And that complicated things. Because this was supposed to be the woman she despised. This was supposed to be the woman she hated.

They might be working together now. But make no mistake about it, the second they got out of here...

Aoife heard footsteps.

Grace looked at her. The mood instantly shifted to something uncomplicated again.

"You hear that?" Grace asked.

Aoife nodded. "They're coming this way."

She tightened her grip around the blade, saw Grace do the same.

"If they come in here..." Aoife started.

"They won't."

"And how can you be sure of that?"

Grace looked around.

Then at the floor. Like she was trying to come up with something. Like she was trying to figure out what to do next.

And then she looked at William's body. "We need to move him."

"What?"

Grace got to the shoulders. "We need to drag him out in the hall. If they find him, they'll go into the room we were in. And then we have a chance to run."

"I'm not sure—"

"Come on, Aoife. Don't fucking dilly dally here. We both want to get out of this. Help me out."

Aoife shook her head, then rushed over to William.

Grabbed his ankles. Tried to lift him, but he was quite weighty, quite hard to shift.

"He's too heavy."

"Oh, don't be a little bitch about it," Grace said. "Come on. Through the door. Just drop him outside. He'll draw them towards the room we were in."

Aoife gritted her teeth, used all the strength she had to drag the body through the door. "I'm not sure about this."

Those footsteps getting closer.

Those voices getting closer.

She stepped out after Grace, William's bleeding body between them, and suddenly felt vulnerable in the corridor. Suddenly felt on show.

"Quick," Grace said. "They're coming."

They dragged him further through the door, over towards the door near the room where Kent was.

Dropped him.

Then they turned around and saw them.

Two men.

Weren't looking yet. Seemed miles away.

But two of them.

Walking up some stairs and heading their way.

"Back in there," Grace said, pushing Aoife.

Aoife tumbled back into the floor.

Saw Grace pull that door shut, right behind her.

She crouched there. Silent. Listening to those footsteps.

Those voices.

"This better work," Aoife whisper. "This better fucking..."

She heard it.

The shouting.

The confusion.

The footsteps turning to jogs.

"What the hell? It's the boss. It's the fucking boss."

Aoife could hear them right outside the door.

She knew they were close. So close. A stone's throw away.

Go look for Kent. Go look for us and go look for Kent. Don't come in here. Don't...

"Why the hell did Wolfy not hear? The fucking deaf bastard."

And then something happened that filled Aoife with total fear.

That made every inch of her body sink.

She saw the handle to the door turn.

And saw the door to the room she and Grace were in start to open.

CHAPTER FORTY

Aoife held her breath as the door to the room she and Grace were in opened, just slightly.

She clutched the knife. Readied herself for anything. She knew what she had to do. She knew there was only one way out of this.

To fight.

She watched that door open even more when she heard something. Time standing still.

The door stopped.

A voice.

"Fuck. They've fuckin' got Kent!"

And in that instant, the door stopped opening.

It swung shut.

Aoife heard footsteps rushing towards the double doors that Kent's body was behind.

She heard them rushing into that room.

And she knew now was the moment.

Now was the chance.

"Come on," Grace said. "Out of here. Right now."

They ran. The pair of them bolted, out the door. Didn't look back to see if anyone was chasing them. Didn't stop to see if anyone was coming after them.

They just ran down that corridor together.

Making a break for the stairs.

She ran towards the stairs, almost reached them when she heard the door swing open.

Heard the voices.

"They're there! Stop 'em!"

"Shit," Aoife said.

Both threw themselves down the stairs, fully aware they were being chased now. Fully aware that there wasn't much time at all. They had to keep going. They had to make a break for it.

They ran down the stairs. Looked around for more steps. Down the next set of stairs, Aoife could hear voices. See movement.

"They're coming from both ways," she said.

They stood there, the pair of them. Right there in this dirty old corridor. Men approaching from upstairs and from downstairs.

They were trapped.

They were...

And then it hit her.

"The window," Aoife said.

Grace turned around. Frowned. "What about it?"

"It's smashed. It's... We can make that drop."

"Are you sure? It looks a hell of a fall."

"Do we have any other choice?" Aoife shouted.

Grace stood there, and she sighed. Nodded. Footsteps getting closer and closer.

"We've got to make a decision, Grace. We've got to make a decision right this second. We can't just stand here. Can't just stay here. We have to get out of here. Right now."

Grace looked at Aoife with a blankness to her eyes. In a way she'd never looked at her before. "Yes," she said. "Yes, we do."

She looked around at the drop.

Then looked back at Aoife.

"Go on. You first."

Aoife gritted her teeth.

Went to run towards the window to throw herself out of it.

And right at the death, she felt something.

A hand, dragging her back.

Yanking her back.

"Not so fast," Grace said.

And then she felt it.

A hot burst of pain in her upper right thigh.

She screamed. Screamed and collapsed to the floor. There was nothing else she could do. The pain. The agony. Growing more and more intense by the second.

She looked up and around at Grace, who stood over her, bloodied blade in hand.

"Maybe they can have their fun with you," she said. "Maybe they can put you through hell. And maybe when they're done with you... I can finish you off."

She looked back as the sound of the footsteps approached.

"They're going to be *really* pissed with you for what you've done to their people."

And then she turned around, stepped out of the window, and disappeared into the darkness.

CHAPTER FORTY-ONE

A oife sat in the chair in the darkness and had no idea how long she'd been here.

Only that she wanted a drink of water. Desperately. She was blindfolded. She couldn't see a thing. Had no idea where she was, only that she was tied to a chair, which she'd been sitting in so long that it actually hurt. She felt weak. Totally exhausted. Her leg, which had been stabbed, ached like mad. Unconsciousness rose and fell. She had no idea what was real and what wasn't real anymore. Even her dreams were doused in darkness.

The only thing she knew was that she'd been here for a long, long time. And it felt like she was never getting out of here.

She hadn't been sexually assaulted. That was a small comfort. Something she'd feared when Grace stabbed her, left her behind. The four men who'd caught up with her—the two from upstairs, the two from downstairs—had been rough with her. They'd punched her for what she'd done. Kicked her. Left her feeling like total shit. But thankfully, anything sexual didn't seem to be on the table, something that relieved her in a horrible kind of way.

Because if what she was going through right now was a relief...

she couldn't bear to think of what it'd be like if things got even worse.

She kept on replaying everything that had happened. Kept on drifting back to that moment. The moment she and Grace reached the open window. The moment she'd told Grace they needed to jump. That they needed to escape. Needed to get the hell out of this place.

Going to jump and then feeling the sudden burst of pain in her leg.

Seeing Grace staring down at her.

Betraying her.

She really believed Grace when she told her that she wanted revenge so dearly that the pair of them were going to get out of this place first before resolving their differences. But she supposed that was another betrayal in itself. Really, the fate Grace had left her to was far, far worse than anything that Grace could do to her individually.

And the horror that worse things were to come kept on haunting her, kept on robbing her of sleep.

But despite all this, despite how trapped she was, how exhausted she was, how weak she was... it was six months ago that her thoughts kept on returning to. What she'd done to Grace's people. How she'd trapped them. How she'd burned them. How she'd gone against the estate's decision and taken matters into her own hands, and all the consequences that followed.

How that one decision of hers had caused everything. Prompted everything.

She thought of her home, burning.

She thought of Max, dying.

She thought of everything that had happened.

And as she sat there, all the desire for revenge drifted out of her.

Because she didn't want revenge anymore.

She deserved everything that came her way.

Everything.

She didn't want to pity herself. She knew self-pity was pointless, and she'd never liked being weak.

But right now, sitting in that chair, in the dark, desperate for a drink, alone, knowing that untold horrors were to come... Aoife felt acceptance.

She'd done this,

She'd caused this.

And she was going to pay for it.

She heard the door swing open again. Or maybe she didn't. Maybe it was in her mind.

She heard footsteps coming her way.

She felt someone drag her blindfold from her—one of the men, the quiet one with the red hair and the mean face and the freckles.

She saw the way he snarled at her.

And then she saw him pull back his fist and punch her.

And feeling that pain, tasting the blood, Aoife didn't feel like it was unjust anymore.

She didn't even fight it anymore.

Because she deserved it.

It wasn't a fraction of what she'd put her people through.

She felt another punch, tasted more blood and felt the darkness surrounding her even more.

CHAPTER FORTY-TWO

Grace looked back at the large, abandoned hospital building where she'd left Aoife, and she had a mixture of emotions.

When she first left Aoife, she imagined her screaming. Imagined hearing her in pain. And she wanted to believe she'd feel good about that. She wanted to believe she'd get a lot from knowing that Aoife would be suffering. In agony.

But the screams hadn't come.

She'd waited a long time. Two days, she'd spent, in the outskirts of the suburb, just watching. Waiting. Occasionally, she swore she saw movement inside and wondered if Aoife was in there. Imagined all kinds of punishment she might be going through, all to try and make herself feel better.

But she didn't feel better.

None of it made her feel better.

All she could think about were the things she'd done.

The ways she'd punished Aoife already.

The ways she'd sought revenge.

And as she lay awake at night, one thing haunted her that

she'd never thought about before. That she'd never once considered.

What if Grace deserved what she'd gone through?

What if her people deserved what Aoife had done?

She felt sick at the thought. Dismissed it, right in an instant. But the feeling wouldn't stop nagging at her.

Because as much as she told Aoife—and told herself—that she wasn't on board with Christopher, that so many of the people there weren't on board with him... she had to ask herself the question, could she have done more to be less complicit?

She pushed the thoughts away as much as she could. Tried to hide from them. Tried to resist them.

But it was in those moments, lying there on the cold dark floor at night, that she thought about what she'd done.

The people she'd watched die.

The people she'd eaten, knowing full well that she was eating another human being.

The opportunity she'd had to stand up. The opportunity so many of them had to stand up and revolt.

The opportunity she'd failed to honour.

She thought about Aoife standing over her and her burning people, and for the first time, she saw it from another perspective.

From Aoife's perspective.

The anger in her eyes.

The rage at what Christopher had done to her people. At what he'd tried to do to her and done to so many others.

She thought about that rage and then thought about her own obsession this last six months, and she felt the throes of guilt beginning to rise up.

What had she done?

She gritted her teeth. Heart pounding. Over to her right, she heard something. The dog, whining. Aoife's dog. Even though she'd been trapped in that hospital, this dog seemed to have taken a liking to her. And she couldn't exactly push it away. Wasn't doing anything wrong at the end of the day.

But just seeing it here, seeing its pathetic, needy little face staring at her... it reminded her of Aoife. And it reminded her of her guilt.

She turned away from the window. Walked over to the back of the room. Sat down, went to lie and close her eyes, when she felt the dog nudge her. Felt it lie there, next to her. Whining just a little.

And having it here, having it so close to her... seeing how accepting it was of her, despite everything she'd done to its people, to its humans... it got her in a way that surprised her.

It let her off.

It forgave her.

It forgave her in a way she couldn't forgive Aoife.

Couldn't forgive herself.

She sat up in an instant. Bolted upright. The dog scampered away a little, back into the corner of the room.

And as Grace sat there, staring out at the building opposite, she knew deep down there was only one place she could go.

There was only one thing she could do.

She didn't know how it would end. She didn't know if she'd regret it. She didn't know a thing.

The only thing she did know?

She didn't want to leave Aoife in that hospital with those men.

Because Aoife was still *hers* to decide what to do with.

She looked at the dog as he stood there beside her, staring out the window.

Then, she took a deep breath.

"Come on," she said. "We've got work to do."

CHAPTER FORTY-THREE

Aoife had no idea how long she'd been tied to a chair in that room.

Only something suddenly jolted her awake.

She was cold. Freezing cold. Kept waking up shivering. Usually, when she opened her eyes, she saw nothing but the suffocating darkness of her blindfold, completely blocking her vision.

But there was something different right now.

She saw a glimmer of... well, it wasn't exactly *light*. But it wasn't total darkness, either.

She squeezed her eyelids together a few times. Head banging. Leg aching like crazy. She wondered if this was some kind of dream. If maybe she'd lost her grip on reality altogether.

She looked ahead and saw the big window before her. It was nighttime. The only light came from the moon, the stars. She could see her breath clouding before her in the cold. She could taste the rustiness of blood on the back of her throat. The blindfold had slipped down her face, just a little.

But enough that she could see.

Just being able to see was a relief in itself. It made her feel more connected. More alive.

And even though for a moment, she'd given up, she felt determined right now.

She felt like her desire to live was alive again.

She didn't know why, only...

She saw movement up ahead.

Someone climbing up through the window.

And when she saw him, she realised right away this wasn't real. It couldn't be real.

Because it wasn't possible.

He stood there before her. Tall. Bearded. Well-built. Smile on his face.

"Hey, Aoife," he said.

She looked at him standing there, and her instinct was to cry. But not with sadness this time. With relief. Relief that he was here. Relief that he was alive. And even if she knew he wasn't real... even if she knew this had to be in her head... he was real enough for her.

"Max," she said.

He just stood there. Smiling. Looking at her like he was just as happy to see her. "I would ask how you're doing. But right now, it doesn't look like you're doing too well."

And she laughed. Despite everything, despite the pain she'd been through, she actually laughed. "You always make me feel better. Always did."

Max's smile widened. A light seemed to have formed around him now. He was so visible. So... clear. "I could say the same about you."

Aoife went to say something. But then her stomach sank. "But you're gone. You're not here. And it's because of me."

Max's face twitched just a little. His smile faltered. His eyes seemed to drop just slightly. Almost like he was mirroring her realisation himself. "I know there's nothing I can say to convince you this wasn't because of you."

"That's because there's nothing *to* say," Aoife said. "I did this. I went against what we'd agreed at the estate, and I caused this. If I hadn't done what I'd done... this wouldn't have happened. None of this would have happened. And you'd still be here."

Max looked at her. A glimmer of pity in his eyes. He shook his head, flat smile to his face. "That's not true, Aoife."

"But it is true. I have to own it. I have to take responsibility for it. I have to—"

"Own it, maybe. Take responsibility for your actions, maybe. But blame yourself for what happened? This could have happened to anyone, Aoife. It could have happened to any of us at any time. You need to remember who is really to blame. For everything. And it's not you. It's definitely not you."

Aoife didn't want to hear it. She didn't want to accept it. She didn't deserve that much.

"You made errors. But then so did I. I made errors with Kathryn. With David. I made so many errors with so many people. And I blamed myself for it. So many times, I blamed myself for it. But you can't let regret define you. You can't let regret haunt you. You just have to let it go. You just have to learn from it. And you just have to move on."

Aoife felt those words deep in her chest, and she cried. Because as much as she wanted to hear them, as much as she wanted them to resonate with her, she knew he was just in her head. So she was hearing what she wanted to hear, in a way.

"You're dead, and I'm imagining you saying what I want you to say," Aoife said.

Max smirked. "It's not ideal, is it?"

"No. No, it's not."

She looked at him standing there, so close but so far away.

And she took in deep breaths of that cold air and let herself sink into the fantasy that there was more to this meeting than a mere dance of thoughts.

"I am sorry for what happened," Aoife said. "It'll live with me for the rest of my life."

"But you can't let it hold you back," Max said. "You can't let it haunt your future. You know that's what I would have said."

She looked up at him, and right then, she felt those words strongly, too.

Because he was right.

Despite everything… she knew Max would never blame her.

She knew he loved her.

Just like she loved him.

"I love you."

"I know," Max said. "And I love you too. But I'm always here. Always. You just have to remember me. Conjure the grumpy bastard up like you're rubbing a genie's lamp."

Aoife laughed again. Cried and laughed. "Look at me. Chatting to a figment of my imagination. I think I've finally cracked."

Max looked at her from afar, and his smile widened even more. "Nah. I'd say you're sounding saner now than you've sounded in a long time."

He drifted, then. Drifted from view. And she wanted to reach out for him. She wanted to get up out of her chair and stop him disappearing. She wanted to get up, and she wanted to fight…

But she knew there was no catching him.

She knew he was drifting away.

She knew he was going.

She watched him fade from view.

Watched him mouth the words that both soothed and destroyed her.

I love you.

"I love you too," she said. "I love you too…"

He disappeared from view.

Aoife gasped, opened her eyes.

She saw what she'd seen before. Darkness. Only not total darkness. Her blindfold was off.

The moon and the stars beamed through the window.

And when she looked up, she saw two men standing over her. Smirking.

"I'm glad you're awake," the cold one with the dead eyes said. "We want you awake. For what's going to happen next."

CHAPTER FORTY-FOUR

Aoife saw the man with the dead eyes walk towards her, and she knew what was coming next.

She could see it in his eyes. That look, predatory. She'd seen it in the eyes of so many other men before. Every woman had seen it in the eyes of so many other men before.

And society before the collapse never used to do a great job of holding them back, especially when they were drunk. Men seemed to be born with this feeling of a God-given right to comment on how a woman looked, with no respect for her boundaries, with no desire other than to get one thing from them before discarding her.

But now, in a world after the collapse, a world where the thin rules and ethics that were already in place had collapsed completely, Aoife knew she was always going to be faced with this, some day.

She felt him put his hands on her shoulders.

Saw the way he looked into her eyes.

Like she was barely human.

And then he pushed the chair back.

She cracked her head against the solid, hard floor. Ankles flailing.

Tied to this chair by her waist, her wrists bound together.

The taste of blood even stronger in her mouth now.

And the pain in her leg burning hot and intense.

She tried to turn onto her side, but she felt trapped. Stuck. Like a tortoise on its back. She tried to pull her wrists free of the ties, but it was no use. She was trapped. Tied to the chair. Wrists tied. Leg wounded. And two men standing over her.

She felt trapped. She felt powerless.

She felt weaker than she'd ever felt.

"You had no right to do what you did," the dead-eyed man said.

And then he kicked her.

Buried a boot right into her kidney.

So hard it made her whole body seize up.

Blood trickling from her mouth, from her bloodied nose.

"You had no damned right to do what you did at all."

Another kick.

Another sharp, agonising pain, right down her side.

Another suffocating blow that she wasn't sure she was going to be able to get up from.

"When we caught you, when we brought you here... that's when you lost your damned right to do a thing to us."

She felt the chair topple over.

Felt herself land on her side, now.

Head spinning.

Ears ringing and blocked like there was water in there. Or blood, more likely.

Vision fading.

She felt the man grab her arm, and at that instant, at that split second, she noticed something.

One of the blades.

One of the blades Grace must've dropped when they'd got out of here, staring right back up at her.

She saw it. And she knew she needed to be instantaneous. She knew she needed to act fast.

"Well, you did what you did to us. And you know what? I ain't gonna be as lenient as the boss was. I ain't gonna hold back."

She felt him grab her arm.

Go to pull the chair back up.

Stretched out for the blade...

The man dragged her up.

The chair upright now.

Him staring down at her. His sour breath covering her face.

And that smirk, too, as his friend looked over like he was officiating things.

The man stared down at her. His eyes on hers at all times. That smile of his widening. He even looked like he was drooling, just a little.

"Any last words before I change you forever?" he asked.

Aoife gritted her teeth. "Yeah," she said.

"Go on. Humour me."

She leaned in, right towards his ear.

"Never leave blades lying around in future."

She cut her wrists free.

Lifted the blade right up.

Swung it into his eye.

He screamed. Let out a cry, blood spurting everywhere.

The man behind him staring on, alarmed, as his friend staggered everywhere, his eyeball burst, his screams rabid.

She yanked herself up after breaking the ties—weak-ass ties— from around herself free.

Went to pull back the blade and stab the other bloke.

"No," he said. And she noticed something. The pistol he was holding. Pointing at her. "Not another move."

As the sound of the man crying and screaming filled the room, part of her just wanted to throw herself at this bloke with the gun and be done with it once and for all. Even if she went down, she went down fighting.

But then she heard something else.

A gasp.

Saw the man's eyes widening.

Rolling back.

Saw him drop the pistol.

Saw him reach for her neck, which suddenly gushed with blood.

She stood there and stared at him as he staggered a step towards her.

Then he fell down, right before her.

Onto his knees, then his skull hit the floor with a thud.

She looked down at him.

Then up, behind him.

Someone was standing there.

No. Not just *someone*.

Someone she recognised.

"Come on," Grace said. Knife in hand. "Let's get the hell out of here. For real, this time."

CHAPTER FORTY-FIVE

Aoife saw Grace standing opposite her, knife in hand, and she felt a sudden surge of rage.

"Come on," Grace said. "No time to stand around and wait."

"You bitch," Aoife spat.

"Hey. A little harsh. I came back for you, didn't I?"

"You stabbed me. You left me to them. You..."

And Aoife realised then that by offloading like this to Grace, by showing how worked up she was about everything, how much it'd got to her, she was actually giving her what she wanted.

Because Grace *wanted* Aoife to be in pain.

She *wanted* Aoife to suffer.

"Fuck you for this," Aoife said. "Seriously, fuck you."

Grace's eyes looked happy. Genuinely happy. "I was never going to leave you here. You didn't deserve to be let off the hook like that. Now come on. Let's get a move on. The other blokes'll be onto us in no time."

She turned around, rushed over to the window, which Aoife realised was smashed, now.

Stopped when she reached it. Looked down, down below.

Aoife tried to limp over towards it but walking hurt. The stab wound wasn't as bad as it could have been, but it still wasn't great. No way she could do any running, that was for sure.

She limped her way over to the window. She could hear footsteps approaching, even though she was deaf in one ear from the kicking she'd had—hopefully only temporarily.

She reached Grace's side, and she wanted to bury that blade into her.

But at the same time... it struck her that she needed a hand right now.

She needed a hand because of her leg wound.

She had to use Grace to her advantage right now.

And there was something else, too.

That sense.

The sense that she deserved what had happened to her.

And that sense that Grace was going to get what was coming to her, eventually.

"Besides," Grace said. "Look down there. I brought a friend of yours to see you."

"You really want me to go first again? Think I'm actually falling for that again?"

"Seriously," Grace said. "Just take a look. Besides. I'm not one for pulling the same trick twice."

Aoife leaned forward, half-expecting another blade to the leg.

But when she saw who was down there, she couldn't quite believe what she was looking at.

Sitting there in the darkness.

Wagging his tail.

"Rex," Aoife said.

"We've got a slight problem," Grace said. "We're going to have to climb down to the next window. The ladder I propped up against the front, it only reached so far. But there's plenty to hold on to, don't worry."

Aoife shook her head. "After what you did to my leg? You really think I'm climbing my way down here?"

"You can do what you damned well want. But do try to stay alive, wouldn't you? I'm not quite done with you yet."

For a moment, Aoife swore Grace winked at her.

But then she walked to the window and dropped down.

Climbed her way down the loose bricks protruding from the side of the building.

Got to the window below, then hopped down onto a ladder and clambered her way down.

"See?" Grace said. "Simple."

Aoife gritted her teeth. She could hear the footsteps of the others approaching. She knew she needed to act pretty damned quickly if she wanted to get out of this.

"Fuck it," she muttered.

She went to climb her way down the side of the window.

Clawed at the loose, protruding bricks.

The cold air blowing against her, icy, biting.

"What are you doing?" she muttered. "What are you actually doing?"

She climbed further down when she heard the voices in the room above. They were in there now. They'd found the two blokes she and Grace had killed. Shit. She didn't have much time left.

She climbed further down, leg aching like mad, arms weak, body totally drained.

Kept on going until she reached the next window.

Until...

One of the bricks.

Going loose, in her palm.

Holding her breath.

Waiting to fall.

And then it holding. Holding just as long as she needed it to.

She climbed further down the side of the window. Dangled her foot down, desperately trying to find the ladder.

"Hurry up," Grace called.

"I'm trying, okay? Would really help if you hadn't *stabbed* me."

She dangled her leg down further, trying to find the top of the ladder, when she felt it.

Felt it right there beneath her.

The ladder.

She was on it.

She could start climbing down it.

She could get away from this.

She eased onto it. Gasping with relief. Then she climbed down it, further and further.

She was almost at the bottom.

She was almost there.

She was almost.

"Fuck!"

She stopped.

Froze.

Footsteps.

Footsteps below.

She could see two men. Reaching Grace.

She could see Rex barking. Kicking back.

She could see the way Grace tried to stand her ground, tried to fight.

And she could see then how these two men wrestled her to the ground.

She looked down at Grace. Right down into those bright green eyes. Saw the way Grace looked up at her. Knowing. Accusing.

And Aoife kept still, in the darkness. Completely still.

She watched as those men dragged Grace away, back inside the building.

She waited until she was absolutely sure she was in the clear.

And then she climbed down that ladder and reached Rex's side.

"Come on, Rex," she said, fussing him, cuddling him, rubbing his fur. "Let's... let's get out of here."

She looked into the darkness of the derelict old hospital.

And then she took a deep breath, turned around, and walked.

CHAPTER FORTY-SIX

Aoife limped off into the woods as night turned to day. But she couldn't stop thinking about one thing. The most surprising thing of all.

Grace.

She looked over her shoulder, back towards the town, back towards where she'd come from. The abandoned hospital she'd escaped. She thought about what'd happened to her in there. How she'd been beaten. And how she'd been so close to being sexually assaulted.

She thought about it, and she thought about Grace, back there with whoever was still alive in there.

She thought of what she might be going through right now. The horror she might be feeling. All because Aoife had turned her back on her, just as Grace had turned her back on Aoife.

The betrayal.

The abandonment.

Why did it feel so wrong when really, it was so right?

Grace had murdered Max. She'd murdered so many of her people. She'd destroyed her home. Left her for dead. Stabbed her in the leg and then gone back for her in some kind of emotional rollercoaster.

And despite all that, Aoife felt this urge. This desire to get to her. This sense that this couldn't be the way things ended.

This weird feeling that Grace didn't deserve this. That the pair of them had already put each other through enough hell as it was...

But no. She couldn't think like that. Couldn't show weakness.

Grace deserved everything she was getting.

She limped further along. Her leg ached like mad. The bandage the blokes had wrapped around it didn't look the cleanest, and blood was leaking through. She just had to hope the wound was superficial and would heal by itself. Just had to hope it didn't get infected. That'd be a real shitter. Killed by a second-rate infection after all she'd been through. Really made her question the point of everything. Whether life even had a point at all.

She thought about Max. How his life ended, so abruptly, so suddenly, so without resolution. Life didn't have neat little resolutions. Maybe Grace was destined to die at the hands of those men, and maybe Aoife was destined to die at the hands of blood loss and infection.

And did either of them really deserve any more?

She stopped. Rex stopped by her side. She checked the bandage. The wound wasn't bleeding too badly, not as badly as she thought anyway. But she was going to have to stop at some point. Going to have to take a breather.

She sat down. Leaned back against a tree. But the tiredness that hit her scared her. Fuck. What if she was losing more blood than she thought? What if infection was setting in already?

What if she was dying?

So she yanked herself back to her feet, afraid to stay still in case she passed out and died, when suddenly a crippling sense of dread hit her.

It didn't matter who'd instigated the horrors that had gone down.

It didn't matter who was more or less to blame.

And it didn't matter that Aoife hated Grace with her fucking life for what she'd done.

She could be the better person here.

She could be the one who rose above all the shit and all the horrors that'd happened.

She could be the better person.

She stared back, right back, right through the trees. Right along the path she'd walked.

She thought about Max.

Thought about her community. Thought about her home.

She thought about what Grace had taken away from her.

And then she thought about what she had taken away from Grace, too.

Just for a moment, she let herself think about that.

Then she swallowed a sickly lump in her throat, and she sighed.

She looked down at Rex.

Then, back in the direction she'd come from.

And as much as her body told her not to do it, as much as her mind told her to hold back, to resist... Aoife walked.

CHAPTER FORTY-SEVEN

Grace felt the man slam his fist into her face and tasted blood.

And at that moment, she didn't care.

She hadn't cared about anything for a long time. Especially didn't care about someone kicking the shit out of her. Her face was a decent target, in all truth, because she didn't feel much pain there anyway.

But in a way, she wished she could feel pain.

Because she'd let that bitch Aoife get one over her.

She'd come back here, stupidly. Come back here to help her out. Well, not to help her... or fuck, maybe it *was* to help her, she didn't even know herself.

But she'd come back here for whatever reason and helped Aoife out of the mess she'd found herself in, only something had happened.

She'd been caught.

And Aoife had stood there on that ladder, staring down at her just like she'd stared down at her when she was in that burning pit, coldness in her eyes, and she'd got one over her, once again.

Another crack against her face. The taste of blood intensifying. She didn't know how long she'd been here, locked in this room. These two men before her, trading punches, again and again, and again. She could hear them saying things. Lewd things. Things about her appearance, about how fucking ugly she looked, about how she was a monster.

And as much as the residual shame haunted her, she just let the words wash through her at this point.

Because at the end of the day, what else could she do?

Sit here. Feel those punches crack against her. Wait for them to abuse them in whatever ways they deemed fit.

All she had to hold on to was her hatred for Aoife.

Her hatred for doing this to her.

But can you blame her, really?

It was that thought she kept coming back to. The thought of her actions, of the things she'd done to Aoife to make her react in the way she had.

Could she really blame her?

Hell. Who gives a fuck?

The bitch wasn't supposed to get one over her like this. She wasn't supposed to have the last laugh. It was supposed to be Grace who had the power, who got her revenge, not Aoife.

But Grace had let her guard drop.

She should never have gone back for Aoife. She should have left her to suffer at the hands of these creepy fuckers.

She should have let them finish her off.

But then that guilt, and that attachment, and...

Another punch right across her face.

Head spinning.

Darkness approaching.

Grace sat there on the chair, and a part of her still couldn't quite believe this was the end. Couldn't quite accept it. This wasn't how her story was supposed to go. She was a clever kid. A bright young girl. She'd had a good life, and she was destined to go far.

And now she couldn't even see herself in that old life.

Now, she didn't even recognise the person she used to be.

The things she'd done.

What would the old Grace think of her?

What would her parents think of her?

What did she think of herself?

Another hit.

More blood.

More darkness.

But this time, something else, too.

A feeling.

A feeling buried beneath all the strength, all the coldness.

A feeling of pain.

Of sadness.

Of longing for what she'd lost.

Of her little brother, Tim, and the play fights they'd have. The running races they'd have by the side of the pond when they were kids.

The happy childhood they'd had.

She thought of it all, and then she took a deep breath through her blocked and bloodied nose and waited for the next punch.

Another crack.

Another burst of blood.

And then, darkness.

CHAPTER FORTY-EIGHT

Aoife saw the abandoned hospital in the distance, and she knew exactly what she had to do.

She knew she was mad. Fucking crazy, even. Her leg was sore as hell, and she was absolutely exhausted. She'd spent God knows how long awake, walking through the woods, finding the supplies she needed to get through, to survive.

And all for what?

To save a woman she despised.

A woman who'd killed Max and destroyed her home.

She might be fucking crazy. But she wanted to be the better person.

She had no idea what she'd do with Grace when she got her out of this place. No idea whether she'd just end up killing her after all.

But in a weird kind of way, she knew Grace was right when she'd said they had business to settle between them.

And that's exactly what they had to do.

She took a deep breath. Looked down the slope towards the entrance to the abandoned hospital. She knew there weren't many scavengers left in that place. Only a couple, maybe a few more.

They'd be manageable. Easy enough to get past.

But still, she had to be careful.

It was dark, at least. It was dark, and that gave her the best cover. The best opportunity. The best chance.

Only there was one problem.

Rex.

She wrapped the lead around his neck and tied him around a tree. Felt so bad doing so, seeing his ears drop, hearing him whine.

"Ssh, lad. Ssh. This isn't the end. I'll be back for you, I swear."

She made sure not to tie the lead too tight. Part of her wanted to know he could slip it if he absolutely had to. If it came to biting it off, he'd be able to, that was for sure.

But she couldn't risk dragging him in there with her. Couldn't risk losing him.

No. This was a mission to handle herself.

She patted his head, ruffled his fur. And as she looked into his big, brown eyes, she felt an air of finality about everything. A sense that this might just be the last time she ever looked into his eyes. The last time she stroked him.

And in a deep sense, maybe that's what she deserved. Maybe she didn't deserve another opportunity. Another chance.

But shit. Whatever she deserved or didn't deserve, she knew what she had to do. Knew there was only one way.

She had to go get Grace out of the grips of those fuckers inside.

At least Grace had a reason for attacking Aoife. For doing what she was doing. For doing everything she had done.

A twisted, messed-up reason that Aoife would never see eye to eye with. But a reason all the same.

These men just wanted to hurt. Just wanted to cause pain. Just wanted to dominate.

But Aoife couldn't allow that.

She took a deep breath, stroked Rex's head again.

"It'll be okay, lad. I'll come back for you. I swear I will."

Then, she stood tall and tensed her fists.

It was time to go get Grace.

And then it was time to settle the score between them.

Once and for all.

CHAPTER FORTY-NINE

Mitchell went to take another swing at the ugly bitch when he heard something creaking from the corridor behind him.

He stopped. Looked around. Probably Dave-o goofing around again. Always liked pulling pranks. Bit of a dick, that one. Mitchell never really liked him.

But he was one of the last ones left. So they had to stick together.

For now, anyway.

He looked back. Back across the dusty, dark room. Over towards that corridor. Come to think of it, Dave-o had been gone for a while now. Which wasn't like, weird in any way. He often snook off and smoked drugs in his spare time. Had a shitty little cannabis plant and a greasy old bong. Absolutely reeked of weed at all times, he did.

But hey. Everyone had their ways of getting through this world.

He looked back at the woman. Or at least what was left of her messed up face, anyway. Her eyes were bruised and swollen over now. Hardly much of a face left.

He could still hear her breathing, wheezing. And for a second, he felt bad for her. Behind that messed-up face, he wondered if she was pretty underneath. Wondered what secrets she had. Hell, maybe he'd stop punching her now. Maybe he'd keep her around, get to know her.

After all, the people her and that other bitch killed?

He didn't like 'um so much. Not really.

They were always dicks to him. Took the piss because he was a bit slow.

But he wasn't slow. Mum always used to say he was special. He was quicker than the rest. Just a different kind of person to the rest of 'um on the planet.

But then Mitchell was pretty sure his mum used to fuck his uncle on the regular, so she wasn't exactly the most sane role model, really.

Hell, even Dad said Young Mitchell was the spawn of incest, once.

He looked at this woman, and he wanted to stroke her bloodied, bruised face. He wanted to look after her. Wanted to care for her. She'd be okay, here with him. Maybe the two of 'um could survive together. Maybe they didn't need Dave-o at all, even though the rest of the folks here knew more than he did about survival stuff. He was good at killing, and he was strong, and that's why they liked him around. He knew that.

But maybe he was cleverer than they all thought.

Maybe he was stronger than they all thought.

He looked back around. Heard those footsteps.

"Dave-o?"

Nothing. Nothing but his voice echoing.

He sighed. Looked back at the woman. She wasn't going anywhere fast.

He grabbed a match, lit a candle.

He turned around again and left the room, headed through

the darkness into the corridor. Regretted it right away. It was so dark out here. Even darker than he remembered.

When he got to the corridor, he stopped.

He couldn't see anyone. Anything.

No sign of Dave-o.

But...

A sound.

A sound, right at the top of the corridor.

Floorboard creaking.

Then movement.

He held his breath. His heart racing like mad, just like it did when Dad used to burn him with that hot poker. Just like it did when he used to punch him again and again and again then make him...

No. He didn't want to think about that.

That movement up ahead.

Had to go check on it.

Had to go see.

"Dave-o? Quit it, pal. You're creeping me out."

He walked down the corridor. Further into the darkness. Every step felt like it was taking forever. He just wanted to get to the end of this corridor. He just wanted to find Dave-o.

Then he wanted to get back to his girl.

He reached the end of the corridor.

Stopped, right by the corner.

Then he stepped around it.

He could see someone standing there in the dark.

They looked tall. About Dave-o's height.

But he was dead still.

Completely still.

"Dave... Dave-o?"

He looked around. Turned and started stumbling towards Mitchell.

And Mitchell realised what it was, then. A prank. A damned prank where he pretended he was some kind of zombie.

"Come on, Dave-o. You really creeped me out there."

But Dave-o didn't stop walking.

"Dave-o?" Mitchell said. Shaking a little. "Stay back, man. Stay back. Or I'll..."

He saw something, then.

Saw Dave-o as he stepped into the candlelight.

He was bleeding.

Bleeding back from between his legs. Right from his private parts.

Naked from the waist down.

Bleeding from a gaping hole where his cock once was.

"What... what happened to..."

And then Mitchell saw something else.

Dave-o's cock.

It was sticking out of his own ass.

He stood there and stared at Dave-o as he whimpered, cried, shivered.

And then he felt warmth behind him. Heard movement.

"What—"

He felt a slice against his throat.

Dropped the candle to the floor.

And as he collapsed down, hand around his choking mouth, the last thing he saw was the woman—the prettier woman—standing over him.

Staring down at him.

As the flames got closer to him, closer to Dave-o, swallowing them up whole...

CHAPTER FIFTY

Grace heard footsteps approaching and braced herself for the next bout of whatever beating was coming her way.

She kept her eyes closed. Didn't really have much say in the matter, in all truth. She'd been beaten. Thumped repeatedly. Her remaining teeth were loose, and she couldn't taste anything but the rustiness of blood.

And as she sat there in this chair, in total darkness, a part of her wondered if maybe she deserved it.

Maybe this was the ending she was always going to face.

Maybe this was what she got for pursuing her vengeance over Aoife for all this time.

And maybe this was what she deserved for getting sloppy. Getting complacent.

She gritted her teeth together and waited for those footsteps to reach her. For the taunting to start. To hear all over again about how fucking ugly she was, how much of a freak she was.

But she didn't hear any of that.

The footsteps stopped. But it felt like there was someone here with her. Like she wasn't alone.

She opened her eyes as much as she could. Squinted through the blood and the tears, towards what little light shone through.

She saw someone standing over her. A figure.

Initially, she thought it must be one of the thugs who'd been beating the shit out of her. Thought some even harsher punishment might be heading her way.

But the more she squinted into the dark... the more she realised it wasn't any of those people at all.

"Yeah," Aoife said. "Surprised to see me?"

Grace felt two things. The same two things she'd always felt about Aoife lately: both a deep, unshiftable hatred and burning desire for revenge. But also a sense of relief. Relief that she was still here. That she still had an opportunity to settle the score with her, if that's what it came to.

A sense of guilt.

"Couldn't leave you to these tossers," Aoife said, walking over to her, untying the binds around her. "It's like you said. Can't exactly let a bunch of men decide our fate when we've got far more to settle between us. Now come on. Let's get out of here."

She sat there as Aoife untied her. And the more she untied her, the more her strength seemed to grow. She realised then she'd given up. She'd lost all hope. And losing all hope had made her start to accept her fate.

But now, seeing there was an opportunity, seeing there *was* a way out... she felt energised. She felt recharged.

"Come on," Aoife said. "That should do it. Now let's get the hell out of here."

Grace gritted her remaining teeth together. Opened her bruised, swollen eyelids even more. She tried to stand, but she was shaky and weak. Tried to stay on her feet. Tried to stay tall, to maintain her composure.

But she just strafed from side to side.

Tumbled forward a little, then backwards.

As much as she wanted to prove she was strong enough, as

much as she wanted to show a display of strength despite every-thing she'd been through... she fell forward to the floor.

Pain hit her this time. A pain she didn't even think she was capable of feeling. Right across her face. Or was she imagining it? Was it all in her head? She didn't know anymore. Whatever it was, she didn't like it.

Because it wasn't just physical. It was emotional, too.

She wanted someone to help her up.

She wanted someone to help her to her feet.

She wanted someone to look after her.

And then she felt it.

A hand against hers.

Aoife's hand.

"Come on," Aoife said. "You need to get up. And we need to get out of here."

Grace turned around. Looked up at Aoife. She could see the bloodied bandage on her thigh. She could see her own bruises on her pale face. And she could see that look of conflicted hatred in her eyes. The same look Grace knew she looked out with.

But she could see Aoife holding her hand, too.

"On your feet. We need to get out of here. Before anything else."

And as much as Grace didn't want this woman lifting her to her feet, as much as she didn't want her help or any shred of her pity... she let her ease her up.

Got to her feet. Stood there, right beside her.

"Where's the dog?" Grace asked. It was the first thing she could think to ask, and she wasn't even entirely sure why.

"He's safe," Aoife said.

"Good," Grace said. "Despite everything... I've grown rather fond of him."

Aoife didn't say anything back to that. Grace wasn't even sure why she'd said it either. All this having the shit kicked out of her business was doing funny things to her.

But the fact of the matter was... she was standing. She was out of the chair. She was free.

And Aoife was right here beside her.

"Come on then," Grace said, her voice shaky, raspy. The taste of blood so strong in her mouth it made her want to puke. "Let's... let's get out of here, then."

Aoife nodded. "That's the spirit."

She walked on, then. Led the way, across the dark, dingy room, over towards the door.

When she reached the door and opened it, she froze.

"Shit," Aoife said.

"What?"

But when Grace stepped around the doorway and looked out into the corridor, she didn't have to ask.

The corridor was filled with flames.

The building was burning.

They were trapped.

CHAPTER FIFTY-ONE

Aoife stared out at the burning corridor and, in a weird way, felt a kind of poetic justice about this whole thing. The flames had spread fast. So fast that she hadn't heard anything, hadn't smelled anything, hadn't even noticed. But they were crawling up the walls of the building. On the ceiling. And on the floor, too.

It must've been from the match. Shitting hell.

She stepped out, Grace by her side.

Stopped right away, the heat too intense.

"Fuck," Aoife said. The smoke catching on her lungs, making her splutter. Fuck. They were stuck in here. They were stuck, and time was running out fast.

"What the hell are we supposed to do now?" Grace asked.

Aoife looked at her, standing there, shaky on her feet. Then back at the dark room behind them both. There was the window, but the drop from this level was too risky, especially when she had a bad leg and Grace had been beaten to within an inch of her life. The ladder they'd used before was gone. There were no doors from the room they were in to the other side of the building.

There was no hope.

She looked at Grace, and on her bruised face and in those bright green eyes, she saw horror. The same horror she'd seen when she'd looked down into that burning circle and seen her looking back up at her. Her blindfold burned away by the flames. The look of fear in her eyes. Of horror. Of pain.

She saw it reflected back at her, and she knew they only had one choice.

"We need to get through the corridor," Aoife said.

Grace shook her head. "No chance we're getting out that way. What about the window?"

"The drop's too far."

"We—we can climb."

"Neither of us can climb."

"We have to climb!" Grace shouted.

Seeing her like this, seeing her so bereft of composure, seeing her so scarred by the flames, by the prospect of facing them once again... traumatised by what had happened to her... she couldn't help pitying her.

"Grace," Aoife said. Not seeing the woman who'd murdered Max. Not seeing the woman who'd destroyed her community. Who'd taunted her and put her through hell.

But seeing a woman who wanted the same thing as her— revenge—and allowed that lust for vengeance to drive her every move.

Grace looked around at her. Lowered her head. Didn't quite look into her eyes.

"I know this isn't easy. And it might just be the death of us. But... but we need to try going down that corridor while we can. I can still see the stairs. And I... I know it's not going to be easy. It might not come to anything. But we have to try. We just have to try."

Grace looked up at her, then. Right in her eyes, just for a moment. "You don't know a thing about burning. You don't know a thing about the heat. About the pain. The agony. And the sad thing? Despite everything I think of you for what you've done... I don't wish it on you. I wouldn't wish it on anybody. And I'm so sorry for putting other people through what you put me through."

Hearing those words, Aoife felt bitterness inside. The knowledge that Grace knew just how much Max would suffer—knew just how much so many others in the community would suffer—and still did it anyway.

But then Aoife had done it, too.

She'd put Grace and so many others through it.

She couldn't take the moral high ground right now.

"It changes nothing," Aoife said. "We need to get out of here. And it's... it's the only way."

Grace looked at her, the flames reflecting against her face, lighting her up.

Then, she sighed, and she nodded as the smoke grew thicker. "It's the only way."

She turned around. Faced the corridor.

And Aoife turned and faced it, too.

She saw the flames on the walls.

The thick smoke growing heavier and heavier, blocking their view of the staircase now.

She felt the heat growing more and more intense.

Saw the flames even dancing along the floor.

And she knew she had no time to wait.

She walked.

Walked towards that heat.

Walked, Grace by her side.

It hit her in an instant. So much hotter. Unbearably so. So hot, she could feel her eyeballs actually drying out.

And it didn't get easier. The air. The air was actually hot to breathe. Impossible to inhale, not just because of the smoke but because of the heat.

So hot it felt like her body was going to set on fire all by itself.

Just another step.

The soles of her feet feeling like they were melting.

The tears on her face impossibly warm.

Keep going. You can do this. Keep...

She looked around.

Saw Grace on the floor.

On her knees.

Panting.

Hyperventilating.

She wanted to keep going. Wanted to leave her here. Wanted to take this opportunity and get out of here.

But she felt that guilt and that pity again.

No.

Be the better person.

You owe her that much.

She walked back down the corridor.

Out of the most stifling heat, but still not much better. The very clothes on her back burning her.

She grabbed Grace. Grabbed her shoulders as she limped along.

"Come on," Aoife said.

"I can't do this."

"You have to do this, Grace. You have to do this."

Grace looked up at her, then. Bloodshot eyes filled with tears.

"I can't go through it again. I can't go through it again..."

Aoife looked around.

Head spinning.

Heart racing.

Then she tightened her hands around Grace's body.

"You won't have to. Because we're going to get out of this."

She pulled her to her feet with all her strength.

Turned around.

Saw flames ahead, even more than before.

Saw them above.

Saw them all around.

And felt the burning growing hotter and hotter and hotter.

And as much as she wanted to believe there was a way out, as much as she wanted to believe she just had to keep on going... Aoife saw reality staring her right in the face, now.

They were trapped.

They were trapped, and they were dying here.

They were burning to death here.

And there was no way out.

CHAPTER FIFTY-TWO

I t all happened so fast.

The stifling heat, closing in, getting more and more intense.

The smoke filling Aoife's lungs.

And that horrible, horrible sense of inevitability that this wasn't going to get better.

It was going to get worse.

Much, much worse.

She thought of what Max went through.

She thought of what Grace went through.

She thought about it all, and she found herself doing something she never expected.

Something she didn't even realise she was doing until she truly focused.

Her hand.

Holding Grace's hand.

Tight.

No way forward.

No way back.

Trapped now.

She went to take a deep breath of that air that felt like it would burn her lungs from the inside when something happened.

A shift.

A shift beneath her feet.

And then falling.

Falling down below.

Falling and then—

Smack.

Against the floor below.

Above, she could see the flames. She could see debris tumbling down all around her. And her body and head ached like mad from the collision with the floor.

But that coolness to the air like stepping in a cold shower.

That coolness and that sudden relief.

Aoife turned over. Her leg and her body aching like mad.

But she'd fallen through to the floor below.

Both had fallen through to the floor below.

But there wasn't much time left.

Soon, the whole building would be on fire.

She turned over and saw Grace lying there. Staring up at the flames above. Traumatised, fixated eyes.

"Come on," Aoife said. "Won't get a better chance than this. We've got to get out of here. Now."

Grace looked around at her.

Then back up at the flames.

Looked right up at them in that way she'd looked up at Aoife, standing above her, six months ago.

"Come on, Grace. It's time. We've got to go."

She held out her hand again.

And again, with some hesitation, Grace took it.

She helped her to her feet. Grace let go of her hand the second she was standing. The pair of them stood there in the corridor, by the huge window.

"I'm guessing jumping's still off the table?" Grace asked, limping alongside Aoife.

"Unless you want to maim yourself even more. In which case, be my guest. Come on. The stairs are just up here."

They limped down the corridor. Fully aware the ceiling was collapsing on them. Fully aware the flames were spreading fast.

And fully aware that if they didn't get out of here quickly, their good luck falling through the fucking ceiling was going to be all for nothing.

Aoife reached the stairs. Limped her way down it, Grace following close behind—

A crash.

The ceiling above, totally caving in.

Hot debris dropping down everywhere.

"The whole building's coming down."

Aoife nodded. "Which is why we really need to get the hell out of here."

She turned. Limped further down the steps. The pain in her leg growing more intense by the second. No idea if she had the strength or the energy to keep going. No fucking clue if she had it in her to get out of this mess.

But she just kept going.

She clambered her way down to the bottom of the stairs.

Went to turn to take the final set of steps.

That's when she saw the man standing there. Right before her.

She hadn't seen this bloke before. Didn't even think there were any left.

But he was standing there, right in their way, blood on his face and a gun in his hand.

"It's over," Aoife said. "This place. Everything. It's over."

The man shook his head. "My friends. My people. You came here, and you destroyed it. Destroyed everything we had."

He lifted his pistol.

Walked a few steps closer to Aoife. To Grace.

"You don't get to walk away," he said. "You stay here, and you burn. The pair of you, you burn."

Aoife stepped back a bit.

Heard another crash.

Flames behind her.

Debris blocking the staircase.

She looked around. Saw that man standing there, holding the pistol.

"You don't get to walk away," he said. "You don't get to walk—"

A crash from above.

A huge chunk of wood and furniture falling down, right on top of the man.

Burning furniture.

His neck cracked.

His gun dropped to the floor.

He disappeared, screaming under the flames.

Aoife stood there. Grace by her side. Watched him. Listened to him.

And as much as she hated these people, as much as she despised them... she found herself pitying him.

Because she knew Grace was right now.

Nobody deserved this.

Nobody.

"Come on," Aoife said, walking on, Grace close by her side. "Let's... let's get out of here."

Grace followed closely.

The pair of them walked out of this burning building and out into the rainy darkness.

They didn't look back once.

CHAPTER FIFTY-THREE

Aoife staggered out of the burning building, Grace by her side, and out into the cold and the dark.

It was raining outside. And it felt such a relief, feeling that rain pour down onto her. Coughing up her lungs, getting rid of all the smoke.

But that cold. That icy cold rain, so fresh against her skin. Soothing, like a balm all over her body.

She felt it enveloping her, and she felt happiness. Total relief, just for a moment.

And then she remembered who was right behind her.

She turned around and looked for Grace.

Something hit her.

Right in an instant.

Like a punch to the gut.

Grace.

Grace was gone.

Aoife stood her ground. Sickliness building inside her. Grace had been right with her. She'd been right beside her when they were leaving the building. Aoife staggered forward for a few seconds, just for some relief and some cool in the rain, and now Grace had disappeared. She was nowhere to be seen.

Two things hit her. First, was Grace okay? She was in a bad way. Maybe she'd collapsed. Maybe she'd got stuck in the building. Maybe Aoife had let her guard drop for a second, and now Grace was dead.

But then there was another feeling, too.

Another sense.

One of unease.

What if Grace was intentionally holding back?

What if she was watching Aoife?

What if she was waiting for the perfect moment to strike?

She looked back at that burning building. At the flames creeping across it. The remains of a building that had stood so proudly for so many years, burning before her eyes.

One thing was for sure.

If Grace was still in there, she was gone.

She looked back and swallowed a lump in her sore, dry throat. Took as deep a breath as she could, her lungs still so sore, every breath so strained. She hated Grace for what she'd done. And she hated herself for what she'd done to Grace and her people, too.

She knew she'd done wrong.

But so too had Grace.

She'd made peace with Grace. That's what this was, right now. She'd made peace with her. And she wasn't going to fight her if it came to it. She wasn't going to continue this cycle of violence. Because she'd seen how far it'd got them both.

She felt guilty for what she'd done.

But she wouldn't feel guilty for anything else.

She looked at that burning building. And as much as she wanted to go back in there, as much as she wanted to check on Grace, to see if she was okay... she knew there was no use. Not anymore. It was already in flames. And wherever Grace was, if she had walked away, if she was waiting to ambush Aoife... regardless of what she'd decided, Aoife had made her decision now.

Vengeance was futile.

She had to move forward.

She had to learn.

She had to move on.

She did walk back, though. Walked back. Checked the surroundings. Looked all around the outskirts of the building for a trace of Grace. Looked at every entrance for a possible way she could get in.

But the flames were too high. And one thing was for sure. If Grace was still here... well. She wasn't still here anymore.

But why did Aoife feel so sad about that?

Especially after everything Grace had done?

She looked back at this burning building.

Looked back at it and let her breath go.

Let her tears fall.

And then she turned around.

She had Rex to get to.

She had Rex to find.

And then she and Rex had a new journey to begin. Together.

She walked away. Kept on looking back. Kept on looking for a sign of Grace. Still unable to understand why she felt so bad about this, especially after what Grace had done.

But knowing deep down it's because she understood.

She understood how much pain hurt.

How much vengeance hurt.

How strong that will for revenge really was.

She understood it.

And she wanted to tell Grace she forgave her for it.

That she was sorry for her part in it, and she forgave her for it.

She walked into the woods. Into the darkness. Into the pouring rain. Closer to where she'd tied Rex up. And a part of her

worried about reaching his leash and finding he was gone already.
Finding it was too late. Finding she was alone. Totally alone.

She walked further into the darkness when she saw something.
The leash.

Dangling from the tree.

Rex was nowhere in sight.

She walked over to it. Crouched beside it. Got on her knees
and cried.

"Please, Rex," she said. "Please."

She rubbed her hand against the lead when suddenly, something hit her.

Rex's collar.

His collar had been unclipped from the lead.

Someone had done this.

She suddenly became aware of a presence right behind her.

Looked around.

Grace stood there, her silhouette illuminated by the
moonlight.

Rex stood at her side.

Grace was holding a pistol and pointing it right at Aoife.

"This is where it ends," she said.

CHAPTER FIFTY-FOUR

A oife stared at Grace standing there with the pistol in her hand, pointed right at her.

Rain lashed down from above. The moonlight silhouetted Grace, making her look even more imposing, even more... well, fucking terrifying at this moment. Aoife could see she was weak. She could see her shaking. See her staggering from side to side.

But she was standing. And she had a pistol, and she was pointing it at Aoife.

And somehow, this really felt like the end now.

"Don't move a muscle," Grace said. Her voice muffled, clearly because of how swollen and beaten her face was. "You've done enough fucking moving."

Her voice was quivery, too. Aoife hadn't really heard her like this. And seeing Rex standing there, by her side, wagging his tail... that felt like the ultimate betrayal.

But she was glad he was there, in a way. Rather that than dead at the hands of Grace.

"Grace," Aoife said. "I came back for you—"

"And more fool you for doing so," Grace said.

"This doesn't have to be how it ends. There's... there's got to be another way."

"You just don't get it, do you? Even after everything. You just don't get it. You sit there and you beg and you try to tell me there's another way? Even after what I did to your people? After what I did to... what was he called? Max?"

Aoife's stomach turned at the mere mention of his name. "Don't say his name."

"I enjoyed what I did to him. I enjoyed what I did to all your people. And I've enjoyed putting you through hell. Because... because you deserve it. You deserve every ounce of it. For what you did."

"I know I deserve it!" Aoife shouted. "I think about it every single fucking moment. What I did to you... to your people... irrespective of what you'd done to us, it was wrong, and I'm sorry. But what you did to us was wrong, too. I know it's not about point scoring... but we're both in this."

"And that's why it has to end like it does," Grace said.

Aoife opened her mouth. She didn't know what to say. Not anymore. "You could have killed me."

"What?"

"So many times. You could have killed me. But you haven't. You've... you've told me it's because you're making me suffer. But I know, Grace. I know. No suffering is ever enough. Not when you've lost people you care about. Lost people you love. And it'll... it'll never, ever be enough. And I know something else, too. It won't bring the ones you love back. I'm sorry, but it won't. But you're putting yourself through this. You're keeping me alive because you don't want to let go. But we can, Grace. We... we can."

Grace stood there, pistol still pointed at Aoife. Shaking in her hand. "I know... I know what my people did was wrong. I know what Christopher did was wrong. But you took away our chance—"

"And I'm sorry for it!" Aoife shouted. Her voice echoing right through the dark woods, the rain lashing down, drenching her.

She stood up. Walked over towards Grace. Not caring anymore. Not giving a shit what it meant for her.

Just knowing it was what she had to do.

All she could do.

"Not another muscle," Grace said.

But Aoife wasn't listening.

"I told you," Grace said. "Not another muscle."

"I don't think you'll kill me," Aoife said.

Grace shook her pistol. "Want a fucking bet?"

"I don't think you'll kill me because I think... I think you see what I'm saying is right. I think you see it too. Just like I do. You won't kill me because... because you know as long as I'm alive, your life still has a purpose. Same reason I... I can't kill you. Because as long as I'm alive, and as long as you're alive... we don't have nothing left. Without each other... we've nothing left to be angry about. And nothing left to live for. And the last thing that binds us to the people we lost is gone completely."

Grace held her pistol right at Aoife. Shaking. Blood trickling down from her bloodied, battered, swollen eyes. "You're wrong," she said.

"Maybe so," Aoife said. "But I... As much as I hate you for what *you've* done. As much as I want you dead for what you took from me. From the lives *you* took from so many people... I won't fight. Because the cycle has to stop somewhere. And it—it stops with me. And if killing me is what you do, then go ahead and fucking do it. But I won't fight anymore. I'll be the one to end this."

Aoife stood there. Totally still. Adrenaline surging, body shaking all over.

Grace staring back into her eyes.

And then Grace stepped forward.

Pushed the pistol right to her forehead.

"This ends with you fighting. This ends with you begging."

Aoife shook her head. "No, Grace. No. That's not how it—"

A crack across her face from the pistol.

Rex barking.

Aoife turned, looked back at Grace.

Another smack.

Right across her face.

Knocking her to the ground.

Grace grabbed her hair. Yanked it so hard she swore she felt a whole clump come out.

So hard that she was looking up into Grace's eyes again.

"You *will* beg. You owe me that much. You will beg."

Aoife shook her head. "I won't beg. And I won't fight. Whatever happens here, happens. But my fight is over."

Grace smacked her across the side of the face again. "I loved killing that bastard, Max."

Aoife felt the pain in her stomach.

She saw him, lying there on the ground.

Heard his cry.

"I saw him shit himself at the end," Grace said. "Saw him shit himself and saw him piss himself."

Aoife shook her head. Tried to push the thoughts away.

"I heard him beg for someone, too. In his last breath. Kathryn, I think. Kathryn. And David. And you."

It was then that Aoife flipped.

She jumped up.

Punched the pistol from Grace's hand.

Swung her over.

Cracked it against the side of her face, again and again, and again.

And then she leaned over and buried it against Grace's forehead.

"Go on," Grace spat. "Go on then. Do it. Kill me. Do it."

And Aoife wanted to.

She wanted to empty that trigger.

She wanted to bury the bullets into her skull for what she'd done.

"Do it!" Grace screamed.

And it hit Aoife at that moment.

The desperation in Grace's voice.

It came together.

"You want me to kill you, don't you?"

"Just do it!"

"You want me to kill you because *you* feel guilt. You feel shame. For what you've done. You've... you've already put me through hell. And now you want me to make you suffer. Because *you're* ashamed."

Grace didn't say anything else.

She just cried.

"I just... I just want them back. I'm... I'm sorry. I'm sorry. I want them back. Kill me. Please. Kill me."

Aoife sat there, over Grace. Rex barking by their side.

And as the rain lashed down on them, she did the hardest thing she'd ever had to do.

She tossed the pistol to one side.

Looked down into Grace's eyes.

"I won't kill you," Aoife said. "There's been enough killing already. From both of us."

She got up off Grace, confident she was weak enough to stay down now.

Walked over to Rex.

Took deep breaths, right into her stomach.

Walked away from Grace, towards the darkness of the trees.

Wanting to turn back.

Wanting to make Grace pay for what she'd done.

But knowing she couldn't.

Knowing it was the worst thing she could do.

She looked down at Rex as Grace wailed behind her, smiled a tearful smile, then took a deep breath.

"Come on, Rex. Let's get..."

The sound of someone standing.

Rushing towards her.

She turned around.

Saw Grace standing there, pistol pointed at her again.

"Grace..."

She grabbed the blade from her side.

And before Grace was upon her, she held it up and buried it into her chest.

Grace fell onto her, spluttering.

She fell forward, the pistol falling from her hand.

She fell onto Aoife, and Aoife felt her world open up beneath her.

Because she hadn't wanted to do this.

She didn't want it to end like this.

But she'd had to.

She'd had no other choice.

Grace staggered to her knees. And Aoife helped her to her knees. Choking blood. Struggling. Falling down.

But not fighting anymore.

Not kicking up any kind of fuss.

At peace.

Aoife lay her down on the forest floor. Lay her down and looked down into those green eyes. Those eyes didn't look up at her with fear anymore. They didn't look up at her in pain.

They looked up at her with the innocence of a child.

Aoife stroked her head gently.

Softly.

Like she was stroking a baby's head.

"It's okay. I'm sorry. It's okay now."

She held her hand.

Stroked her head.

Rain lashing down.

Grace staring up at her, eyes not wavering from her.

"I'm... sorry. I'm... sorry."

Aoife felt resistance.

She felt reluctance.

She wanted to make her pay.

Wanted to make her suffer.

But then she took a deep breath and let it all go.

"I forgive you," Aoife said. "I'm sorry for what I did. I forgive you. It's okay now. It's okay."

She held on to Grace's hand in the pouring rain for what felt like forever.

As her grip loosened.

As her body went limp.

As her last breath crept from her lungs.

Then silence.

CHAPTER FIFTY-FIVE

Aoife looked out at the remains of the estate and took a deep breath.

It was a gorgeous day. Felt like spring was approaching. The air felt warmer to breathe. It hadn't rained in days, which made for a nice change. She still felt soaked from that night a week ago when she'd fought with Grace. When Grace had died in her arms.

She thought about that day all the time. That moment all the time.

Not with any kind of sense of justice about what had happened. Not with any pleasure at getting revenge on the woman who'd destroyed her home and killed the most important person in the world to her.

She thought of it with sadness and regret.

Sadness that things couldn't have worked out differently.

And regret that the cycle had ended exactly as Grace predicted.

With one of them dead.

She took another deep breath of that mild air. Rex sniffed around at the grass by her side, wagging his tail. She could hear birds singing in the trees. Feel the sun's warmth shining down. A winter's day still, sure. But a sign that spring was coming. That better days were coming.

Another year without power.

She saw it all laid out before her, and she felt a deep sense of dread. The thought of going into a new year in this life, completely alone but for Rex. Her worst fear of all. The loneliness. Having to start all over again.

But then she felt that dread dissipate.

She felt that reluctance to bond with someone new dissipate.

She had to be willing to let people in.

She had to give whoever was out there a chance.

It wasn't going to be easy moving forward. Definitely wasn't going to be easy moving on. She wasn't sure she ever would, not truly.

But she'd be damned if she wasn't going to try.

She looked at the crosses there in front of the estate. In front of her. She'd put seventy down in total. Fifty to remember the people of her estate. But also some extra to remember those of Christopher's people who'd lost their lives, too.

Because as bitter as it felt, as mixed as her emotions were about it... she knew it was the right thing to do.

Christopher's people had done horrible, unforgivable things. But some of them weren't bad people. They were afraid. They were cowards. They got behind a leader doing awful things instead of standing against him and rebelling because they genuinely didn't see another way for themselves.

And Aoife knew she was wrong for taking their lives. She knew she was wrong for not giving them another opportunity to be better. Another chance to be better.

She looked at one of the crosses and thought of Grace. Losing her brother. Being disfigured beyond recognition. The hatred she must've felt. That lust for revenge, all along.

But deep inside it, an inability and an unwillingness to kill Aoife. Because having Aoife alive gave her life purpose.

And without Aoife, she was as good as dead.

That was sad. And as much as Aoife detested Grace for the things she'd done... deep down inside, she understood.

Didn't empathise. Didn't relate.

But understood.

She let the thoughts of Grace and Christopher and all their people drift from her mind, and she thought of her own people. She thought of Hailey and her bossiness. She thought of Sam and how joyful he was. She thought of Geoff... Yeah, even Geoff was just lost. She hated him for his betrayal. For his role in what happened to their people.

But he was just dangling onto hope, too.

Could she really blame him for that?

But above all those people, it was one person she went back to thinking about. That same person, every single time.

Max.

She thought about Max, and she felt a knot in her stomach. She closed her eyes. Took a few more deep breaths and felt like he was here, in her presence. Imagined he was right here, in front of her. Listening to her every word.

"Hey," she said. "Me again."

A silence responded. A breeze. No words. Nothing.

But a sense that he was listening.

A sense that he was out there.

Or right here. In her heart.

"I know it's kind of cheesy. But I... I made you something."

She reached into her pocket. Pulled out a little wooden boat she'd carved over the last couple of days. It was shit, far worse than the many efforts she'd mocked Max for. But still... it was something.

"I know it's crap," she said, walking over to the cross in front of the estate. "If you were here, you'd be taking the piss out of me for it. But yeah. It's my first effort. So give me a break, you grumpy old git."

She laughed. That silence responded, again. An emptiness. And yet... like there was something there. Like she wasn't totally on her own.

"I wanted to take it to your house. But I realise... your heart was right here, in the end. With everyone else. You changed. You... you changed, and you taught me how to change, too. And I'll never forget that lesson you taught me. Never."

She looked up again. Tears welling in her eyes. Rex sitting beside her, staring on, panting.

She felt that instinct to apologise kicking in. To apologise for her part in what had happened. To apologise for her role in everything.

But then she tightened her jaw and held her breath.

Because Max wouldn't want her apologising.

It was all just the flow of experience.

It was all just life and death in this crazy, unpredictable world.

And she'd learned a lesson. She'd learned a hell of a lesson about conducting herself in this world. And she'd learned a lesson about revenge, too. Revenge and its value. Its worth.

She'd learned that it got her nowhere.

All it brought was pain.

It never brought satisfaction. Not at all.

Not even the times when her revenge had felt justified. Like over her ex, Jason.

It never brought peace.

She stood up. Walked back from the crosses. Looked at them, lined up against one another. Every single one of them a reminder of what had happened. A reminder of the futility of revenge.

And a reminder of the many lives that had been lost.

Lives that didn't need to be lost.

A mistake that would never happen again.

Because she'd always be the better person from this point on.

Always.

She took another deep breath of that warm air.

Looked at the crosses.

At the crosses of the fallen on both sides.

Grace's cross.

Max's cross.

She looked at them all, tensed her fists, and then let her breath go.

It was time to move forward.

It was time to walk on.

She looked at the remains of the estate—the place she'd called home for a year—one final time.

"Goodbye," she said. "And... and thank you. Thank you for everything."

She looked back at the crosses, thought of Max.

Looked at the wooden boat.

The metal motorbike model.

And the little pouch of porridge oats, too.

"I love you."

And then she turned around with Rex by her side, and she walked into the woods, out of the sun, and into the unknown.

* * *

SOMEWHERE IN THE DISTANCE, not far from Aoife, the electricity sizzled, the lightbulbs burst to pieces, and the power sparked back to life again.

END OF BOOK 4

After the Darkness, the fifth book in the Survive the Darkness series, is now available on Amazon.

If you want to be notified when Ryan Casey's next novel is released—and receive an exclusive post apocalyptic novel totally free—sign up for the author newsletter: ryancaseybooks.com/fanclub

In memory of Pebbles, the best little dog anyone could wish for. Rest in peace. 2009-2021.

Printed in Great Britain
by Amazon